The only light inside was a single one-hundred-watt bulb. Without it, the barn was completely dark. When Maris climbed into the pickup and nodded, Lauren pulled the string to turn the light off. Maris carefully squirted the light gray interior and the floorboard with the Luminol solution. She was already sweating underneath the safety glasses and respirator as she carefully examined the interior of the pickup on the passenger side. Luminol, a colorless liquid, reacts with blood to form a compound that glows in the dark and makes it possible to see bloodstains or patterns of bloodstains invisible under normal conditions. Luminol could detect wipe marks, handprints or other bloodstain patterns.

Seeing nothing of interest, Maris turned on her flashlight. She shifted on the seat and sprayed the driver's side. Again, there was nothing that resembled blood on the seat, door panel or floorboard. A grease smudge on the door luminesced slightly, but she had recognized it as grease earlier. It was negative for blood when she checked it to be sure.

She sprayed the steering wheel and had almost given up when she noticed a small smudge that appeared to be a fingerprint or thumbprint. She marked the location with a felt marker and turned the flashlight on as she opened the door of the truck. Lauren turned on the overhead light.

Maris removed her respirator and said, "One possible bloody fingerprint or thumbprint on the steering wheel. I want to photograph it, if I can. Don't know if the pictures will work or not, but we'll see." She shrugged. "Can't catch the calf, if you don't throw the rope."

DEVIL'S LEG CROSSING

THE 1ST MARIS MIDDLETON MYSTERY

BY KAYE DAVIS

THE NAIAD PRESS, INC.
1997

Printed in the United States of America on acid-free paper
First Edition

Editor: Christine Cassidy
Cover designer: Bonnie Liss (Phoenix Graphics)
Typesetter: Sandi Stancil

Library of Congress Cataloging-in-Publication Data

Davis, Kaye, 1956 –
   Devil's leg crossing : A Maris Middleton mystery / Kaye Davis.
       p.   cm.
   ISBN 1-56280-158-9 (p)
   1. Lesbians—Fiction. I. Title.
PS3554.A934925D48   1997
813'.54—dc21   96-45483
                                                                         CIP

To Lynda Ann,
for putting up with me all these years
and, most of all,
for understanding and believing in me.

To Dianne,
who gave me a gentle shove
at the right time in the right direction.

ACKNOWLEDGMENTS

My gratitude to Barbara Grier and Naiad for giving a first-time author a break. Special thanks to my editor, Christine Cassidy, for her patience and excellent advice and to Sandi Stancil for assisting a rookie.

About the Author

Kaye Davis is a criminalist in a Texas Department of Public Safety regional crime laboratory with eighteen years experience. Her areas of expertise include the analysis of drugs, the determination of blood alcohol content in DWI cases, the examination of paint samples and the comparison of shoeprint and tire track evidence. She has testified in court over three hundred times and has participated in numerous crime scene investigations.

Kaye is a native Texan and lives in the Dallas area with her partner of sixteen years and two dogs, Trooper and Dispatcher.

Chapter One

Cool, smooth hands touched her flushed cheeks. She welcomed the fragrance of her lover's favorite perfume. It was Mary Ann, and she was young with soft brown hair, thick and rich. She sat on the side of the bed in a pale blue gown, and Maris saw the outline of her breasts through sheer material that exposed only the slightest impression of her nipples when she turned toward her. Maris pulled herself upright and crossed her legs. She reached to touch Mary Ann's breast and to caress her hair, but Mary Ann caught Maris's hands and held them tightly.

1

"Maris, you've got to pull yourself together. I've been gone almost eight months now, and you've got to go on living. You can't work all the time," she whispered softly.

Maris heard Earnhardt, her border collie, whine.

"Hello, Earnhardt," Mary Anne said. Squeezing Maris's hands, she leaned closer and added, "I can't stand to see you like this — this unhappy, this lonely. It's time to let go. Don't worry, you won't forget me. I'll always be part of you. Please don't stop living because of me. I love you too much to see you suffer. Go on with your life!"

Maris struggled to consciousness. Earnhardt, whining with concern, stood with his front paws on the bed and licked the hot, salty tears on her cheeks. She was instantly nauseated and jumped out of bed, pushing Earnhardt aside. She tangled her foot in the sheet in her haste to reach the bathroom. Earnhardt scurried out of the way as she raced down the hallway into the bathroom, arriving barely in time. Afterwards, when there was nothing left inside, she sat on the edge of the bathtub and pulled a hand towel from the rack. She wet it with cold water from the tub's faucet and pressed it against her feverish face.

Earnhardt nuzzled her uncertainly. "I'm fine, fellow," she said, holding the cool towel to her face. "God, the dream was so real; I thought she was here. It was a dream, wasn't it, Earnhardt?" Only the small night light was on, but she could see the black and white collie cock his head to the side and raise

2

both ears attentively. She felt better, but was suddenly thirsty. Still dizzy, she stumbled into the hallway, turned left and crossed the sunken living room into the kitchen.

Lord, what a jackass she'd made of herself last night. It was her first night out to the bars since Mary Ann died. At least, her first Saturday night out for a real date. And what a wonderful impression she'd made in her debut. Kathy would never introduce her to anyone again.

She hoped that Kathy and Lynn weren't too upset with her. She barely remembered them driving her home. Unfortunately, she clearly remembered telling Kathy how beautiful she was and asking her to leave Lynn. What a way to repay the two friends who had stayed by her side throughout the whole ordeal — at the hospital, during the funeral, as she sold the house. Honor and integrity, always important to Maris, had eluded her last night, and she was profoundly disappointed in herself.

She poured two glasses of water and added ice to one. In the second glass of water, she scooped sodium bicarbonate from a five pound plastic jar and added a powdered aspirin preparation. She carefully carried her two glasses into the dark living room and sat down in her recliner. The digital clock on the VCR read three a.m. It must have been early, but not early enough, Maris thought, when they brought her home from the bar. Kathy was Mary Ann's best friend, and after Maris and Mary Ann became lovers, they often spent time with Kathy and her latest girlfriend. Kathy and Lynn had been together for almost three years, and Maris, like a fool, tried to break them up last night.

3

The thought made Maris's stomach flip and her head pound even harder. Maris liked Kathy from the first meeting and joked about running after Kathy should Mary Ann ever have the poor judgment to leave. Somehow, to Maris's constant amazement, she and Mary Ann were together for almost ten years. Until death do us part, she thought.

It had been so damned fast. On New Year's Eve, Mary Ann was sick with a sore throat, and they laughed about it as they canceled their party plans. Too quickly, her sore throat turned into laryngitis followed by pneumonia. It was not until she was hospitalized that the quacks discovered advanced throat cancer. Twenty-eight days into the new year, Mary Ann was dead. Just like that, Maris thought. Just like that, everything changed.

She sipped her water slowly. Too much, too fast, and she'd be sick again. Earnhardt put his head on her leg, and she stroked his neck. She drained the bicarb mixture and hoped that it would stay down long enough to do some good.

She mercifully fell asleep, awaking to find dawn breaking. It was seven thirty-five, and she was surprised at how good she felt. She dressed in workout shorts and a T-shirt. A good workout would sweat out the rest of the poison, she thought as she unlocked the sliding glass door on the back side of the living room. The door opened to reveal a small laboratory with scientific equipment neatly arranged around the outer walls. A black counter in the center of the room served as a work station with glassware on one side within easy reach and a large, open examination area on the end.

Before her life changed, Maris had been a forensic

chemist with the Texas Department of Public Safety Crime Laboratory. When Mary Ann went into the hospital and they found the cancer, Maris requested an extended leave of absence. She wanted to stay with her. The state, having no "significant other" plan, turned down her request. So, she quit.

After Mary Ann died, Maris sold their home, took out her state retirement and used the insurance money to buy a large duplex on an acre in an older section of Allen, a small town thirty miles north of downtown Dallas on Highway 75 between Plano and McKinney. She chose the site for the location and city regulations that didn't present any zoning problems. Doing much of the work herself, she turned half of the house into a laboratory. One back bedroom, adjacent to the laboratory, became a combination computer room, record-keeping room and workout/weight room. She added an outside door, solid metal, and a foyer with a small desk where she could receive evidence from law enforcement agencies. The door had a mail slot with a chute attached to a locked metal bin. Police officers dropped small items of evidence into the slot when she was not available to receive them personally. She installed an expensive steel vault for evidence storage, and an alarm system for the living quarters and the lab. When she received her DEA license allowing her to legally handle controlled substances, she officially opened the doors of Middleton Forensic Services.

She derived most of her income from the analysis of confiscated drugs and the examination of blood for alcohol content in DWI cases. These quick and easy analytical procedures allowed her to pay the bills, but her specialty and passion was crime scene investiga-

5

tion and evidence collection. As a generalist, trained and experienced in more than one area of scientific expertise, Maris offered basic serological testing on blood and other body fluids, DNA typing using PCR, and trace evidence examinations on hairs, fibers, paints, shoeprints and tire tracks in addition to her crime scene expertise. In May, four months ago, she began receiving cases and, after working twelve and fifteen hours a day, was doing better financially than she had expected. She hoped, with the right combination of luck and hard work, eventually to add another chemist to handle the blood alcohols and drug cases, freeing her to handle the other work.

She forced herself through a quick and vigorous workout, despite a lingering weakness from too much to drink. Her workout routine was one of the few constants held over from her old life, and she was in good shape. She stood five feet ten inches tall with a strong athletic build and low body-fat ratio. Her dark brown hair was wet with perspiration when she finished the weight lifting and started her twenty minutes on the treadmill. She finished her session with a tiring five miles on the exercise bicycle followed by a cooling down series of stretching exercises.

In the shower afterwards, she wondered about the dream, or was it a dream? It seemed so real, and she felt different — no less lonely, and no less sad, but perhaps less empty. Last night's drunk may have served a purpose, she thought, as she dried off and quickly dressed.

As she grabbed her keys, Earnhardt looked at her expectantly, his lazy right ear drooping in contrast to his erect left ear. "I'm hungry, fellow. How about you?"

He answered with a single bark and the nails on his dancing white feet clicked rapidly on the beige tile floor in the foyer as she unlocked the dead bolt on the front door. She set the alarm and locked the door behind them. Earnhardt bounded ahead to the almost new two-tone blue Ford pickup. She had bought it before Mary Ann died, not realizing how her life and employment situation were about to change.

Once on the road, she rolled down Earnhardt's window, and he happily hung his head into the wind. Mid-September, the sky was a cloudless radiant blue and the warmth from the morning sun promised a hot Sunday afternoon. At McDonald's, she ordered a large coffee and two sausage biscuits, one for her and one for Earnhardt. He waited patiently for her to eat and then picked his breakfast from her fingertips as she broke off small bites.

The weather made her think about the convertible, a 1970 Olds 442 with a big block 455 engine. Mary Ann gave it to her, when she turned twenty-nine, for her thirtieth birthday. She knew it would take them a year to refurbish it, and it had. They finished the job just in time to celebrate Maris's thirtieth birthday, July tenth. Restored to original matador red with a white vinyl interior, the Oldsmobile was an eye-catcher with a throaty rumble and lightning speed. They enjoyed it for two and a half years before Mary Ann died. Maris had driven the convertible only once since Mary Ann died — from her former home to her new combination house and laboratory where she had parked it in the two-car

7

garage, removed the battery and tried to forget about it.

On impulse, Maris stopped at a parts store and bought a new battery. At the flower shop next door, she ordered a dozen yellow roses for Kathy and Lynn. She couldn't remember the woman's name, or she'd send roses to the victim of her ill-fated date. After careful thought, she wrote a short note of apology to Kathy and Lynn and sent it with the flowers.

Chapter Two

Maris replaced the battery on the dusty red convertible and changed the oil. She was pleased when the engine fired on the second try. On another day, she'd change the transmission fluid and anti-freeze. She devoted the morning to cleaning the interior and washing and waxing the exterior. Afterwards, she and Earnhardt drove to the beer store and bought a six pack to go with the steak in the freezer that she looked forward to cooking outside. She thought she might take the rest of Sunday off to relax and watch the Cowboys play at three o'clock. She rarely took the time anymore to watch a game.

The convertible looked and felt good. Maris considered cruising the Crossroads to show it off but decided to drive home. Surprised to see a white Ford Taurus parked in the driveway and someone sitting on the front porch, she hit the garage door opener and pulled the convertible inside. Closing the door behind her, she went to meet the unexpected visitor. Maris was startled by the striking, drop-dead beauty of the woman who met her halfway. She smiled at the flowing red hair as the woman's flashing green eyes almost took her breath away. She looked instantly familiar, but Maris couldn't recall the name or place. The redhead wore neatly creased khaki trousers with a short-sleeved red and green plaid button-down shirt and a plain brown belt.

"Hello, Maris Middleton?" she asked, and Maris almost gasped. Her voice, Kathleen Turner low-pitched and provocative, caused Maris to stumble over Earnhardt.

"Yes, I'm Maris," Maris said, trying to use her deepest, most businesslike voice. She had always been disappointed in her own voice. She thought she sounded like a fifteen-year-old kid, and, to her irritation, it grew higher pitched the more excited or upset she became.

"I don't know if you remember me," she said, with the hint of a drawl, when it hit Maris.

"Mount Carmel, in Waco. I remember you," Maris said.

How could she forget a woman like this? During the investigation after the deadly fire destroyed David Koresh's Branch Davidian compound, she saw the striking redhead, in FBI coveralls, surrounded by a large group of fawning men. That night, she called Mary Ann and bravely announced that she had fallen in love with a beautiful redhead. Mary Ann had, as always, only laughed. She knew that Maris was all hat and no cowboy when it came to illicit affairs, and she was right.

"I'm sorry, I remember you, FBI, but I can't recall your name," Maris added. Earnhardt, usually reserved with strangers, jumped on the redhead's leg. "Get down, Earnhardt! Mind your manners, boy." Maris slapped her leg to call the dog back.

"I'm Lauren O'Conner," she said, shaking hands with Maris.

"It's good to see you again. How about a cold beer?" Maris said, holding up the six pack of Miller Lite.

"Thanks, a beer sounds good. That's some convertible you have. What is it?"

Maris told her. "I haven't driven it since . . ." She paused. "In a while. Earnhardt and I washed and waxed it today." She stepped onto the porch, opened the door and turned off the security alarm. "That's Earnhardt," she said, pointing as he ran into the house. "Come on in."

Maris noticed, as Lauren slipped past her, that the redhead was shorter by about three inches and slightly built with a small waist and shapely hips. She handed Lauren a Miller Lite, gesturing to a stool at the breakfast bar. Maris kept a beer for herself and put the remaining cans in the refrigerator. Early this morning, she'd have bet that she'd never drink another one, but it tasted good.

She let Earnhardt outside into the fenced back-

yard and pulled out the bar stool next to Lauren.
"Now, what can I do for you?" Trying not to stare,
she inhaled the subtle fragrance of perfume and
became acutely aware of the woman sitting just a few
inches away from her elbow.

"Alan, at the DPS lab, told me you'd opened your
own business. I remembered him from Mount Carmel
and called to ask for the name of a private forensic
consultant in the area."

"Why do you need a private lab? You've got one
of the best facilities in the world at your disposal,
even if they've had their problems lately." She
recalled recent allegations of evidence-tampering made
by one of their own agents. "Why do you need me?"

Lauren's shoulders drooped. "I'm assigned to the
Chicago field office but I'm on a leave of absence. A
week ago last Friday, my sixteen-year-old niece disappeared from her home. At first, my sister thought
she ran away, but I never believed it. We were close,
although I didn't see her very often, and she'd have
called or come to me." She paused for a sip of beer.
"I wasn't satisfied with the police investigation so I
flew to Texas to find out what happened. I had to do
something. Waiting in Chicago was driving me crazy."

"If you find something that indicates a law has
been broken, will your people help you?"

"They might, if the local police requested it. For
now, I want a crime scene specialist with an independent lab, someone close and immediately available.
If I find important evidence, I want an expert to help
me collect it properly and, if necessary, analyze it
quickly. The FBI lab has a large backlog in most
areas. I know independent labs are expensive, but I'm
willing to do anything to find out what happened to

my niece." Lauren seemed close to tears. "I need advice on this. It's ... it's just different when someone you know is involved."

"I know," Maris said as she got up to retrieve a pen and pad from a table in the living room. "Tell me everything you know. Where it happened, so forth. I can't tell you exactly what my help will cost since the price varies according to the type of analysis performed, but I can give you some ballpark estimates. For an investigation, I charge by the hour." She wrote some figures down on the pad and handed it to Lauren.

Lauren smiled, and Maris had to grip the bar to keep from falling off the stool. "You should at least charge more per hour than a plumber," she said.

"I'm slow, so it works out," Maris teased, thinking, Honey, I'd almost pay you to let me help.

"My niece, Karin, lives with her mother and stepfather in Pierce. Do you know where it is?"

"Sure, it's between here and Tyler, maybe an hour and a half away."

"She went to a football game the night she disappeared, and her stepdad picked her up in town about midnight to take her home. He says that she went straight to bed, but Saturday morning she was gone. Her bed didn't appear to be slept in at all. My sister was sick that night and stayed at home. She didn't see Bobby Joe bring Karin home."

"Do you suspect him of something?"

"No, nothing concrete, but he was, as far as we know, the last one to see her before she disappeared. Of course, someone could have been waiting in her room or outside her window and forced her to go somewhere. I don't know. I've been in Pierce with

Irene and Bobby Joe since Friday evening. They're both distraught. Irene isn't eating or sleeping, and Bobby isn't much better." She paused. "Can I have another beer?"

"Sure, I'll get it, go on." Maris slid off the stool. She slipped two more beers from the plastic ring on the six pack.

"Thanks, I've been so keyed up. I need to relax and talk this through with someone . . . regroup," she said before taking a long drink. "The police claim not to have found anything, but they also said they'd searched her room. If they did, they didn't do a very good job. I found a bloody pair of panties folded inside a small box buried in a drawer with her school mementos. Under her bed, inside a nylon workout bag, I found a blouse with a large amount of blood covering the front of it. I'm puzzled. The panties look too small to be hers. I don't understand why they'd be hidden where they were if they're related to her disappearance. I decided to have them analyzed to see if it could be her blood, but I don't have any of her blood for a known sample."

"We'll start by finding out if it's even human blood. Then we'll decide what to do."

"How long will it take?"

"Do you have the blouse and panties with you?"

"Yes, in the car."

"Go get them. We'll get the paperwork done, and I'll start. It's after three, so I can tell you something by seven or eight o'clock, if it's human. If it doesn't react to the anti-human by then, we'll have to let it go overnight to be sure of the results."

"You'll miss the Cowboys game. Hasn't it already started?"

"What makes you think I care about the Cowboys?"

"Oh, I just guessed you might be interested. I'll be right back."

"Don't worry about the game. I'll listen to the radio, or catch the highlights on the news tonight. Bring the evidence into the lab, through the sliding door. I'll start getting things ready," Maris said as she pulled her keys out of her pocket and headed toward the laboratory door.

A few minutes later, Lauren came in carrying a sealed brown paper sack with her initials and the date written across the seal. Maris smiled approvingly. Whether this evidence was important or not, both she and Lauren would make sure that their handling methods and the chain of custody were beyond reproach. The football game played on the radio quietly as Maris had Lauren complete a form detailing the evidence submitted and what she wanted done with it. Maris gave the evidence and paperwork a laboratory case number that would allow her to track the evidence and the paperwork associated with it, including her bill.

Maris read the submission form and looked up quickly. "Your niece's name is Karin Beauchamp?"

"Do you know her?"

"And her stepdad is Bobby Joe?"

"Right, Bobby Joe Beauchamp."

Maris sat down on the stool by the examination table. "Did he ever work for DPS as a license and weight trooper?"

Lauren looked concerned as she nodded. "Yes, about ten or eleven years ago before he married my sister. He quit to start his trucking company."

"I remember him. I'd only been working in the DPS laboratory for a few months when it happened. He resigned, but it wasn't exactly voluntarily. I have to tell you what I heard. Some of it's just rumors, but it could be important."

"Then you better tell me."

"He had an affair with a recently divorced secretary who worked in the building. Her ex-husband found out and went to the Major, the regional commander. He told the Major that he suspected Bobby Joe of molesting their seven-year-old daughter. Some people seemed to think, until Bobby Joe's ex-wife came forward, that the story was fabricated for the secretary's ex-husband to get custody of the kids. Bobby Joe's ex-wife said that she divorced him because she caught him fondling their daughter. She hadn't pressed charges because she was afraid it would be his word against hers, and he was a DPS trooper. A doctor examined the secretary's daughter and said there was some evidence of sexual activity, but nothing definite. They submitted some vaginal swabs from the little girl, but we didn't find anything. Maybe nothing happened, or maybe too much time had passed since the incident. DPS encouraged him to resign, and he did."

"Oh God," Lauren said. "Karin was about six when he married my sister."

"We don't know if he's guilty of anything, but it may explain the panties you found in Karin's room."

"They look like children's panties, but how would a child know to keep them?"

"I don't know, unless she didn't want her mother to see them. We'll know more after I finish the tests." The telephone rang before Maris could open the paper sack with the panties. "Excuse me," she said as she grabbed the receiver.

"Thanks for the flowers, but you didn't have to send them," Kathy said.

"I was an absolute jackass last night, and I'm sorry. I hope Lynn isn't mad at me."

"She wasn't too pleased with you last night, but she understands. I don't think you'll get a second date with Sandy."

"She deserved better. Tell Lynn that I felt fortunate to wake up this morning without a broken nose or black eye."

"Lynn wouldn't do that." Kathy laughed. "Are you watching the game?"

"No, not yet. I've got the radio on, but I'm not paying attention to it. I've got an emergency case to work."

"Thanks for the roses, and don't worry. Everything's fine on this end. Talk to you later."

"Wait, before you go," Maris said. "I drove the convertible today. Earnhardt and I even washed and waxed it."

There was a pause, and Kathy said, "I'm glad. I think that's great. Wait until I tell Lynn."

Maris told her good-bye and hung up the phone. "Time to get started," she said, pulling on a pair of latex gloves and opening the paper sack. She was relieved that Lauren didn't ask about the call, but she could feel her curiosity. Maris tore off a large sheet of white butcher paper and spread it out on the examination table.

"What time should I come back?" Lauren asked.

"What?" Maris said, thinking about the evidence. "Oh, are you going back to your sister's house tonight?"

"No, I don't want to stay there after what you told me. It might be better if I grabbed a motel room nearby." Lauren shrugged. Her words were almost lost in a loud clap of thunder, and she and Maris both jumped in surprise.

"Damn," Maris said. "I have to let Earnhardt inside. He goes crazy in this weather. Why don't you stay here? This will only take a couple of hours, then I'll cook us a couple of steaks, and we can talk about the investigation."

"I don't want to be any trouble," Lauren said, twirling a long strand of red hair.

"Nonsense, you can baby-sit Earnhardt for me," Maris said, smiling. "Take the hallway from the living room and turn to your right. There's a spare bedroom and bath. Help yourself to anything you need. You can watch the game, and tell me how it goes."

"Okay, if you really don't mind, I'll take you up on it."

"Good, it'll be fun."

As Lauren left to let Earnhardt in, Maris removed the panties from the small box inside the sack and carefully unfolded them. A dried bloodstain, the size of a fifty-cent piece, was present in the crotch area. It appeared to be well preserved, but if the panties really did belong to Karin Beauchamp, the blood must be several years old, too old to respond to normal blood-typing procedures for the ABO blood group or other tests for enzymatic genetic markers. The stain responded weakly to a presumptive test for the presence of blood, proving only what they already suspected — an old bloodstain was present. Maris cut out a small portion of the sample with clean scissors and set it aside for other tests.

Using an ultraviolet light source, she examined the panties for the possible presence of semen. A small area in the back portion of the crotch fluoresced. She attempted routine testing procedures to determine if it was seminal fluid. The results were inconclusive, possibly due to the age of the stain.

Proceeding to the next item, she carefully lifted a white blouse from a smaller paper sack. The blouse had a large round neck embroidered with red flowers to match the flowers around each of the short sleeves. Dried blood spread across the front of the blouse, but no holes or tears were present to indicate a wound in the chest area, and the blood spatters didn't appear to be consistent with a head wound from a gunshot or blunt instrument. It looked like the blood had been poured on the blouse. She made notes of her observations and took pictures of the panties and underwear after she made labels with the case number, date, her initials and the exhibit number.

After a presumptive test confirmed the presence of blood, she cut samples out of the blouse and extracted them in a saline solution. She removed a small round plastic petri dish with agar from the refrigerator that she would use for the Ouchterlony method to determine if human blood was present. The species determination of a bloodstain requires an immunological procedure involving the reaction of the blood sample in question and the antihuman serum. Fresh human bloodstains would react within three to four hours; an older stain might take twenty-four hours.

She cleaned her work area, stored the reagents and locked the evidence in the vault. After washing her hands thoroughly, she returned to the living room. Lauren slept on the couch with Earnhardt curled close to her feet. Sleep relaxed the worry lines around her eyes and mouth, and Maris was touched by her beauty.

Lauren stirred and asked, "Finished?" Turning to sit upright, she flipped her shoulder-length hair away from her face and smoothed the curls with one hand.

"Who won the game? I lost track on the radio," Maris called from the kitchen, trying not to let Lauren see how much she was affecting her. She took two steaks from the freezer.

When Maris dropped into her lounge chair, Lauren said, smiling, "To tell you the truth, I'm not really much of a football fan. In fact, I know almost nothing about it, but I did get in a good nap. Sorry, I can't tell you who won."

"I reckon that's all right. Did Earnhardt drive you crazy with his tennis ball?" Maris nodded to the tennis ball on the couch near Earnhardt's front paws. At the mention of the b-word, Earnhardt lifted his head and thumped his tail.

"We played a little catch. The rain made us both sleepy. How in the world did he get his name?"

"Earnhardt, black number three, the Intimidator." Maris paused and laughed, as Lauren obviously did not know. "Goodwrench Chevrolet." She laughed again. "I suppose you're not much of a NASCAR fan either."

Lauren smiled and shook her head.

"He's named after Dale Earnhardt, our favorite driver in the stock car races. We used to watch all the races..." Maris glanced involuntarily at the photograph of Mary Ann on the mantel above the fireplace.

Lauren stood and walked over to the picture. She picked it up and looked at it closely. "You must have loved her very much," she said softly. "What happened?"

"I did love her very much. She died of cancer, suddenly with almost no early symptoms, except for a slight cough, and no warning it was that serious." Maris sighed.

"She was very pretty and much too young. I'm sorry." Lauren carefully returned the photograph to the mantel.

"Thank you. How did you know?"

"About you?" Lauren laughed as she sat back down next to Earnhardt. "I knew the first time that I saw you at Mount Carmel. Don't tell me that you didn't notice me."

"I noticed. I thought, or hoped, that you might be gay, but you had all those men around you." Maris smiled and raised her eyebrows. "I wasn't sure."

"You know how the FBI is. I tried to be cool."

"And DPS. I'm surprised that the FBI sent someone down there from Chicago."

"My undergrad degree is accounting and I specialize in white collar crime. They were hoping we'd recover some of David Koresh's financial records. We were interested in how he financed his arsenal and whether there was any hidden money. We were hoping to find a tie between the Davidians and a couple of other radical groups we were watching, but most of his files were destroyed. I ended up sifting debris with everyone else. I'm just glad I wasn't on the team that had to dig the bodies out of the bunker."

"That was a gruesome job," Maris agreed. "A local mortician was hired to transport bodies to the Tarrant County Medical Examiner's Office. He came out one day at lunch when only a handful of us were still on site. It was so fucking muddy they couldn't get the hearse close to the bodies. We spent the lunch hour hauling body bags across a couple hundred feet of ankle-deep mud."

"I hated the mud after those days it rained. And the Porta Potties. One of those things was slanted and so muddy I thought I would slide out and flash the guys before I got my pants up." Lauren laughed.

Maris grinned. "I wasn't originally scheduled to go. Most of our chemists were at a convention in Corpus Christi, and they needed me to stay in the lab. Plus, I was just recovering from pneumonia, and I don't think they wanted to expose me to the dust and ashes."

"I don't know which was worse, the dust before it rained, or the mud afterward."

"I don't know either, but I was furious I couldn't go. Finally, I did get to go two days after the fire. The Texas Rangers asked for me. They were in charge of the investigation and were having trouble getting the evidence inventoried and logged in with a proper chain of custody. No one wanted to do it. The evidence was brought from the compound to a couple of metal buildings closer to the road. It was hard work with long hours. We still had evidence to take care of after the others quit for the day. Most of our chemists wanted to work up at the compound where the CNN cameras could find them, and Lord forbid that the DPS lab order anyone to do anything they didn't want to."

"Digging in the grime wasn't that much fun."

"None of it was a hell of a lot of fun. There were some who did an excellent job and worked themselves into near exhaustion, but there were others who should have been sent home. They wanted to be able to say they were there, but didn't want to get dirty or do any real work. We also had some lab personnel who thought the chemists assigned to evidence would be most likely to testify if the case went to trial, and they didn't want the pressure of a high-profile case. After Ranger Wayne Coffey got in a shouting match with one of our finest, he went to the Ranger Captain and I was ordered to Waco. The Captain said he wanted someone who would handle the evidence properly and testify in court anywhere, anytime . . . I guess he couldn't find that person so he sent for me."

Lauren smiled. It pleased Maris to see her smile. "I have a feeling he found the right person."

"Were you there the day they found the floor safe?"

"No, I don't remember that."

"They found this floor safe, charred but still locked, and turned it in to us. Damn, I was hot, tired and dirty. This bastard in a clean, gray pinstriped suit walks by and tells me that he wants the safe opened. I didn't know who the hell he was, but his attitude pissed me off. I told him if he wanted the fucking safe opened he could by God go find some fucking tools and open it himself. He turned and marched out of there in a huff. I figured he'd gone to call Reno or the President. Wayne Coffey started laughing. I got tickled. We laughed until tears rolled down our cheeks. Then we decided that we might as well open the safe. What if there was a million dollars in there? What if it was Koresh's master plan? We scrounged up a metal rod and a hammer and started beating the hell out of it. Before we knew it, this crowd had gathered around us and began making wild predictions about what could be inside. Several video cameras were rolling while we struggled with that damn safe. They were shouting encouragement to us and free advice about how to open it. Finally someone brought Wayne a three-pound sledge hammer and, while I held the metal punch, he smashed the lock. We opened the safe door and it was completely empty. Not even a speck of dust was inside. The crowd gave a collective groan and shuffled away."

"Sounds like your job was much more interesting than picking up burned bullets and sifting through ashes," Lauren said.

"At least I got to see almost everything that came out of the compound." Trying to sound relaxed, she asked, "Are you seeing anyone?"

She was relieved when Lauren shook her head. "No, we broke up about three months ago. The life of the FBI made it too difficult."

Maris went back into the kitchen to look out the window above the breakfast bar. Since she added the lab, there were no outside windows in the living room, and she sometimes missed the view of the backyard. "It looks like it's stopped raining. Let's fire up the convertible and me, you and Earnhardt will go buy some more beer? When we get back, I'll cook the steaks."

"Sounds good to me. Maris, I'm glad Alan sent me to you. You may be just what this confused and depressed FBI agent needed."

And you, Maris thought, as she grabbed her keys and whistled for Earnhardt, may be what this ol' depressed dog and chemist needed.

Chapter Three

Reading the results of the tests on Lauren's evidence, Maris remembered last night's steaks, beer and conversation. She enjoyed it so much that she didn't even read the test results until this morning. Did she feel a mutual attraction, or was it wishful thinking? She forced herself to return to the evidence.

The blood on the panties was human, but the blood on the blouse didn't respond as human blood. Maris unlocked the freezer and looked through her samples to test for animal blood. She didn't have a lot to choose from, but she could test for fish, chicken, goat, bovine, deer or rabbit. She prepared another Ouchterlony plate and set it aside to read in twenty-four hours. She decided to freeze the samples that she had removed from the panties until she talked to Lauren and they determined what to do next.

For the next few hours, she worked quickly and efficiently, analyzing a stack of crack-cocaine cases submitted by a local narcotics task force. The crack, cocaine base, was clean and easily analyzed and identified, and she completed a case every thirty to forty minutes. She was sealing the last case when the telephone rang.

Maris felt her pulse quicken when she heard Lauren's seductive voice. "My brother-in-law agreed to let us search his truck. I talked to the police again this morning. I don't know why he's just now telling me what he knows," Lauren said impatiently. "Officer Bennie Wright tells me that he saw Bobby Joe pick up Karin at the all-night convenience store. It was their agreed meeting place. Bennie says that Bobby Joe was drunk, but he wanted to give him a break. He told him to let Karin drive home. Bobby was offended and got angry, but decided he would rather let Karin drive than get a DWI."

"Intelligent of him," Maris said, taking notes as she talked.

"Bobby Joe says that it's an old grudge against Bennie, nothing to do with Karin. Irene was asleep when they should have arrived home, and she can't verify that Karin actually made it in that night.

27

She'd taken some strong pain medication for a migraine and says she didn't even wake up when Bobby Joe came to bed."

"You want me to examine the truck and look for blood. Luminol the interior and the bed?"

"It might tell us if something happened to her on the way home. Bobby Joe has a barn where we can do it."

"It has to be pitch dark or we won't see the Luminol glow when it reacts — if there's any blood present," Maris said, taking more notes.

"I think it'll be dark enough. Come to Bobby Joe and Irene's house." Lauren gave Maris directions to the Beauchamp place, three and a half miles outside of Pierce.

"I'll be there in about two hours. I've been working on the panties and blouse. The blood on the panties is human, but the stain is too old to react to conventional blood testing procedures, such as ABO typing and enzymes testing. The blood on the blouse is not human, and I'm doing more tests." After reviewing the directions, Maris hung up the telephone.

Maris found the Beauchamp house, a sprawling ranch house of cedar logs, without incident. A Dodge pickup truck, a blue and silver one-ton dually, was parked in the side of the house in front of an old barn. Maris turned into the gravel drive and stopped next to the Dodge. A Pierce black and gold police car was parked in a circular drive next to Lauren's rented Ford Taurus. The Dodge pickup bed was dirty and appeared to be well used. There was a partial bale of hay in the back along with an assortment of tools scattered around a fifth-wheel trailer hitch. The

28

filth and clutter contrasted sharply to the pickup's clean and shiny body, and the chrome gleamed in the bright sunlight. Despite the appearance of hard use, Maris knew that the pickup was not very old, probably a 1996 model.

Looking for Lauren, Maris turned her attention to the cedar log house. She was impressed. It faced north toward the road with a wide wooden porch, complete with two bench swings, extending three-quarters of the way around it. The manicured fescue lawn, green even in winter, was bordered by several tall pine and oak trees. A pile of evenly cut firewood sat neatly stacked in a wooden rack on the east side of the house near the gate to the backyard.

Maris was halfway to the porch when Lauren met her. Maris's heart skipped a beat when Lauren grabbed her hand and squeezed it quickly. "Thank you for coming," she said. "The Chief and Bennie are inside. I invited them over."

"The Dodge, is it Beauchamp's pickup?"

Lauren nodded. "He still consents to the search, but he seems to be nervous. I don't understand any of these people," she said, tossing her red hair angrily.

"Why? What's happened?"

"The police seem interested, but not overly concerned about the whole case, and my sister is aggravated with me for even suggesting the search. The police have been looking for Karin since she disappeared, but it's like they don't have a plan."

"They may not have a plan. Things like this don't happen out here very often."

Lauren crossed her arms and turned away. Maris reached out to put an arm around her shoulder.

"Come on, now. It'll be fine. Let's get started. Maybe we'll find out something important. Come over to my truck and sign a few papers. If you can, I'd like you to get Beauchamp to sign a release form. Since we don't have a warrant, I want to make sure that I have his permission to use the Luminol. It leaves a slight mess when it dries."

Lauren signed the papers for Maris and said, "I'll tell the guys that we're ready to start."

While Lauren took the other papers into the house for Bobby Joe to sign, Maris took her 35-millimeter camera out of its case and hung it around her neck. She was dressed in a pair of dark blue coveralls, with *Middleton Forensic Services* printed in large white letters. The coveralls were covered with numerous pockets where she placed her tweezers, markers, labels and sample envelopes — things she normally needed during an investigation. Since her wallet was in her right hip pocket, she used the left one to carry a small notebook and a pen.

Slowly, she walked around the pickup. She noted the pickup's license plate number and wrote a brief description of the truck. It was an expensive pickup, she thought absently, a Dodge Ram 3500 one-ton with dual rear wheels and a Cummins diesel engine. She paused in the back and noticed some blue fibers hung on the fifth-wheel trailer hitch in the pickup bed. She would take a closer look at those later. She missed it the first time around the truck, but on her second trip she noticed a small dent on the edge of the passenger-side front quarter panel. There was nothing unusual about the dent itself, but a small piece of torn fabric, stuck near the headlamp, attracted her attention. She made a mental note to examine the front of the truck more thoroughly. She made a third trip around the pickup taking photographs and jotting down her observations.

Lauren was not back yet, and Maris waited impatiently. Hands on her hips, she looked toward the house and saw a woman she assumed to be Lauren's sister in heated conversation with Bennie. Lord, with Bennie Wright on the case, no wonder Lauren was unhappy with the police investigation. His evidence was always screwed up when he brought it to the lab. He never had his paperwork filled out, and the women in the lab hated him. One refused to accept his evidence and made one of the men take it. She wondered what they were arguing about.

Not wanting to stand and wait, Maris returned to the dent on the front bumper with some clean tape. She pulled a section of tape off the roll and wrapped it around her fingers. Carefully, she pressed the sticky side on the top portion of the dent. She then placed the tape on a clean white card. She continued in the same manner until she had covered the entire damaged area. The last piece of tape picked up some small brown specks. Could be blood, she thought as she stuck the tape on another clean white card. She labeled, dated and initialed all of the cards before she slid them inside a manila envelope. Using a pair of small tweezers, she recovered and secured the piece of torn fabric. It appeared to be thin cotton — like a T-shirt. It probably wasn't important, just part of the cloth used to clean or dry the pickup. She kept it anyway, remembering her personal rule of evidence collection — better to have it and not need it than to need it and not have it. She was sealing the envelope when Lauren returned.

"He signed everything. The Chief and Bennie will be out soon. The Chief's an old friend of Bobby Joe's."

"I saw Bennie on the porch talking to your sister."

"You know him?"

"Sure, I know both him and the Chief. Chief Wilkes is a good man, but I've never trusted Bennie. What were they talking about?"

"I don't know. Here's the keys. We can put the truck in the barn and shut the door. It should be dark enough."

The barn door was open, and Maris pulled the truck inside. From her Ford, she retrieved her respirator to protect herself from the Luminol fumes. She handed the camera to Lauren to hold and grabbed her spray bottle. As they were about to shut the door, Chief Ray Wilkes, huffing and puffing after the short walk from the house to the barn, waddled toward her with a grin. Bennie, smoothing his neatly trimmed mustache, followed behind. His scowl was as evenly creased as his crisply starched uniform.

The Chief extended his hand and said, "Hello, Maris, heard you had your own lab. Good to see you."

"Good to see you too, Chief. Hello, Bennie," she said to the tall officer behind him.

He nodded in return. Maris pulled a pair of gloves out of her pocket and pulled them on with a snap. "If you want to watch, come on inside and close the door."

The only light inside was a single one-hundred-watt bulb. Without it, the barn was completely dark.

When Maris climbed into the pickup and nodded, Lauren pulled the string to turn the light off. Maris carefully squirted the light gray interior and the floorboard with the Luminol solution. She was already sweating underneath the safety glasses and respirator as she carefully examined the interior of the pickup on the passenger side. Luminol, a colorless liquid, reacts with blood to form a compound that glows in the dark and makes it possible to see bloodstains or patterns of bloodstains invisible under normal conditions. Luminol could detect wipe marks, handprints or other bloodstain patterns.

Seeing nothing of interest, Maris turned on her flashlight. She shifted on the seat and sprayed the driver's side. Again, there was nothing that resembled blood on the seat, door panel or floorboard. A grease smudge on the door luminesced slightly, but she had recognized it as grease earlier. It was negative for blood when she checked it to be sure.

She sprayed the steering wheel and had almost given up when she noticed a small smudge that appeared to be a fingerprint or thumbprint. She marked the location with a felt marker and turned the flashlight on as she opened the door of the truck. Lauren turned on the overhead light.

Maris removed her respirator and said, "One possible bloody fingerprint or thumbprint on the steering wheel. I want to photograph it, if I can. Don't know if the pictures will work or not, but we'll see." She shrugged. "Can't catch the calf, if you don't throw the rope."

Lauren handed her the camera and, at Maris's direction, went to the Ford pickup to find a tripod and some high-speed recording film. It was difficult to photograph the Luminol reaction since the pictures had to be made in total darkness.

After snapping several frames using different camera settings and exposures, she told Lauren to turn on the light, and she moved the camera and tripod to a safe place. The stain on the steering wheel gave a positive presumptive test for blood, but there was an insufficient amount for further analysis.

Maris quickly made a sketch of the steering wheel and a few notes on the results. Assuming that the stain was blood, it might not mean anything. Beauchamp, or someone else, had probably cut his hand while working. She knew there would not be enough detail on the print for identification purposes, but it dawned on her that the size of the print might be important.

In her truck she found a plastic bottle with some amido black. Often used to visualize and enhance bloody shoeprints, it reacts with blood, and some other substances, to produce a black stain that can be photographed under normal lighting conditions. Using a ruler as a scale, she changed the film in the camera to 400 ASA and photographed the stain on the steering wheel after spraying with amido black.

After that, Maris dropped her spray bottles and flashlight into the pickup bed and climbed in. She used a pair of tweezers to pull the blue fibers from the trailer hitch and placed them into a small yellow envelope that she carefully labeled. She slipped the envelope into her pocket and gestured for Lauren to once again turn off the overhead light. She quickly sprayed Luminol over the bed of the pickup. There was a large stain near the tailgate that appeared to have an impression of fabric pressed into it. The pattern was bright in contrast to the dark paint. Maris marked the location and removed her mask.

"Turn on the lights, Lauren," she said, wiping sweat away from her nose and chin. She was careful to let the sweat drop over the side of the pickup bed onto the barn floor. "Ya'll see that stain?"

Lauren and the officers nodded positively. Curious, they gathered around the back of the pickup. "What do you think it is?" Lauren asked.

"A fabric impression, maybe?" Leaning over the area with the stain, Maris noticed a dark brown crusty material in the lower valley between the ribs running up and down the bed of the truck.

"Looks like blood," Maris said, testing a small area of the stain. "And it may be enough to type." She removed another envelope from her pocket and labeled it. With a scalpel, Maris scraped the brown flakes into the envelope.

"This could be where blood seeped through a tarp or sheet. That would explain the fabric pattern in the stain," Lauren said.

Before Maris could reply, the Chief said, "Oh, hell, he probably went hunting and killed a deer or something. Maybe he slaughtered a calf. That'll be his story anyway."

"If he shot a deer, it's out of season. There should be enough blood in the scrapings to determine if it's human or not," Maris said. "He'll have to come up with a better story than that. I think I'll take a picture of it."

Lauren handed her the camera and tripod and more high-speed recording film. Maris replaced the

400 ASA film with the high-speed film for the Luminol photograph. She sprayed the stained area and nodded to Lauren to douse the light. She quickly snapped the pictures.

When she was finished, Maris gathered up her equipment and returned to her truck with the others close behind her. "I'll examine the photographs after they're developed to see if I can determine any new information, and I'll also look at the fibers from the truck. You know how this works — anything I can tell you will be limited without a possible source for the fibers to compare to the ones we found."

"I would have expected more blood in the cab if there'd been a struggle?" Bennie said.

"If it happened inside the cab," Maris said. "Especially if she was bludgeoned or shot. Something like that would have produced enough blood for spatters. I don't think anything like that happened, not inside the truck. The bloodstain on the steering wheel could be from an unrelated cut on the driver's hand."

"Or," Lauren added, "something could have happened to Karin outside of the pickup and, either intentionally or accidently, she was killed, the body was wrapped in a blanket or tarp and hauled away in the back of the pickup."

"I find it hard to believe that Bobby Joe would hurt that girl. So what if they argued? She was a teenager. I think he'll have an explanation for this," the Chief said.

"Maybe. We'll know more when I finish the tests."

"Yes, then we can move on in another direction," the Chief said. "Bennie, tell them what you've got."

"I talked to the friends, Jennifer and Heather, that Karin was with at the football game. After the game, they went to Devil's Leg Crossing to meet some boys, Brian Blake, Jack Trevor and Gene Simmons. They stayed there until the girls had to leave to take Karin to the convenience store to meet Bobby Joe. Brian Blake is Karin's boyfriend, and the girls say that she sometimes would climb out of her window to meet him late at night. He's a real weirdo, but he claims that he didn't see Karin again after she left with the other girls just before midnight."

"What was Karin wearing when she was last seen?" Maris asked.

"Jeans and a sweatshirt, according to the girls," Bennie said.

"Irene's been checking her clothes closet to make sure. Let me go get her," Lauren said, trotting toward the house.

The officers and Maris walked over to the side of the house, and Maris, glad for the break, leaned against the woodpile. Wishing she had something cold to drink, she absently played with the bark on the firewood and noticed some blue fibers scattered over the logs. Bennie and the Chief walked several feet away to smoke a cigarette and watched intently as Maris removed several of the fibers, although technically she did not have permission to search the firewood. Using one of the last envelopes in her pocket, she dropped the fibers inside.

"What do Karin's friends think about her disappearance?" Maris asked as she labeled the envelope and waited for Lauren and Irene.

"They don't think she ran away. They're suspicious of Brian." Bennie shrugged.

"We've looked all over the county for the body," Chief Wilkes said as he lit another cigarette and inhaled. "Bennie's spent a lot of his own time and gasoline looking during his off hours. The Sheriff's loaned us men to help look, but we've had no luck. We've posted bulletins with other agencies, but so far, nothing."

"We both think she's dead," Bennie said. "I hate to be blunt around her family, but I have a bad feeling."

Lauren walked out of the house followed by another woman. Older than Lauren, Irene had a sad, weathered appearance, made worse by the thin lines around her mouth and the deep creases in her forehead.

Lauren introduced Maris and Irene.

"I hope you don't mind, but I removed some fibers from over there," Maris said, pointing to the woodpile behind her.

Irene seemed surprised but said, "Fine, anything that might help find Karin, or explain what happened."

"What can you tell me about the clothes that she might have worn that night?"

"I think that she was wearing jeans and a Pierce sweatshirt with the school mascot on the front. She had an almost new pair of Reeboks, and I can't find them."

"School colors are yellow and black?"

"That's right. The school mascot is the Pierce Tiger. She's in the pep squad, but the girls usually changed out of their uniforms before leaving the stadium. Her uniform was in Bobby's pickup." She paused briefly. "If that's all, I'll be inside. I want to stay close to the telephone." With her head down, she returned to the house.

Maris looked at Lauren, and Lauren answered the question. "I looked at the uniform and found nothing unusual. It confirms what witnesses already told us — she rode in the truck with Bobby Joe. We still don't know for sure if she made it home."

"Look at the blue fibers on the woodpile. They look like the fibers I found in the pickup bed," Maris said, walking over to the stack of wood.

"Interesting," Lauren said.

"I took a sample." Looking around, she added, "I can't think of anything else I need to do here, can you?"

Lauren shook her head, and Maris returned to her truck while the Chief and Bennie talked to Lauren.

Maris packed her equipment and organized the samples that she had collected. She removed the film from the camera and placed it in a small box with the samples. When she heard the police car driving away, she waved good-bye to the two men. She smiled at Lauren as she approached the truck. "What now?" she asked.

"I don't know." Lauren sighed. "I think I'll see if I can catch some of Karin's classmates at school. This is a small town. All of the kids know one another." She looked at her watch. "It's almost four o'clock. If I go up to the school, I should be able to catch the end of football practice. Maybe the kids will talk to me more openly without the local gestapo present."

"Bennie does seem like that type, doesn't he?" Maris laughed as she closed the tailgate on the pickup and locked the camper. She held the box with the samples and film. "I'm sure those football boys will be more than happy to talk to you when they see your red hair and green eyes." Catching a glimpse of moisture in the corner of Lauren's eyes, she added, "Are you all right?"

"I'm fine, just tired. And it's hit me that all of us are talking about her in the past tense." Maris squeezed Lauren's shoulder encouragingly, and Lauren asked, "Is it still okay if I stay with you? I don't want to stay in that house. Bennie is suspicious of Brian Blake, but look at all the evidence we found."

"Remember, it's all circumstantial. Wait for the results before you jump to conclusions. Bobby may have killed a calf or deer."

"I know, Maris. I only wish we could find her."

"I do too," Maris said. "And yes, you are welcome to stay with us. Earnhardt and I are enjoying the company. I'll give you an extra key later."

"I keep thinking about the last time I saw her, almost two years ago. We drove to Houston for a four day weekend. We stayed next to the Galleria and spent the weekend shopping and lying around the pool. We bought new dresses and wore them out on Saturday night to a swanky seafood restaurant. She acted so grown up. I let her talk me into a strawberry daiquiri with dinner. We had a blast. She made me promise to fly her up to Chicago for a couple of weeks during the summer. I never did."

"Maybe you'll still get the chance," Maris said, wanting to believe it was true. She felt a surge of desire as she backed out of the gravel driveway. Lauren, watching from the front of the barn, looked small and vulnerable standing there alone, and Maris wanted desperately to hold her.

Chapter Four

Fresh out of the shower, Maris stepped into a pair of blue nylon sweats and pulled a Texas Tech T-shirt over her head as the doorbell rang. She caught herself hurrying to the door excitedly. Slow down, be cool, she reminded herself.

She opened the door, and Lauren stepped into the entryway. "See you made it," Maris said before she realized that Lauren was almost in tears. "What happened?" She reached out and steadied her.

"You won't believe what I found out after you left."

They went into the living room. Lauren dropped onto the sofa after tossing her purse onto the coffee table. Maris leaned on the arm of the sofa and waited expectantly.

"I talked to the football players, and they were all eager to help. One of them dated Karin for about a month this summer until she became involved with someone else."

"Brian Blake, our weirdo boyfriend?"

"No, that's the kicker. It's Officer Bennie Wright. The football player, Cory something, says that Bennie Wright is always chasing teenage girls. He dates them a while and then finds another one. Parents think he's concerned about the youth in town because he patrols the teenage haunts and talks with the kids. Cory says what he really does is hustle the girls. He insists that Bennie has gotten at least one girl pregnant and drove her to Dallas for an abortion, but he won't say who the girl is. He thinks he saw Karin riding in Bennie's patrol car the night that she disappeared."

"What about the boyfriend, Brian? I was under the impression that she'd dated him for a long time."

"I don't know. Either Brian doesn't care about her other boyfriends, or he's just a close friend to Karin. Cory says that her relationship with Brian was strange. Apparently, when he and Karin went out sometimes Brian would show up uninvited, as if he followed them."

"Sounds like you need to talk to Brian and the other girls yourself. Maybe Brian was more jealous than he admits?"

"Can't trust the local police now, that's for sure." She looked at Maris and smiled. "You look like you

43

just had a shower. Maybe that's what I need. Texas Tech, that where you went to school?"

"No, but I'm a Lady Raider fan anyway. Do you know what they say about Tech?"

"No, what?" She tilted her chin up and toyed with a strand of her red hair.

" 'Texas Tech is where men are men and women are champions!' "

"I thought that was true everywhere."

"It's because of their women's basketball team . . ." Maris's voice trailed off when she saw Lauren's puzzled expression. "You really don't follow sports, do you?"

"No, not much," Lauren said, rubbing her neck. "I think I'll hit the shower."

"You'll feel better. I felt like I was covered with dust. Want something to drink?"

"Yes, later, and I'm starving. It's early. Let's go out for dinner. I'll hurry."

Maris quickly discarded her sweats and T-shirt for a pair of black, sharply creased Wranglers and a white, equally starched and creased Western shirt. She added her black eel boots and a matching black Western belt and spent more time than usual on her hair before giving up.

"Well, Earnhardt, what do you think?" she said looking down at the black and white dog waiting patiently next to her feet.

She heard Lauren turn off the water in the back bathroom and felt her color rise as she imagined Lauren reaching for a towel to dry her lithe, smooth body. Grabbing her wallet and keys, Maris started down the hallway. Lauren's door was cracked open a few inches and Earnhardt used the space to nose his way inside, further opening the door. She heard him bounce his tennis ball across the carpet into the bathroom. Earnhardt, you sorry devil, she thought, and contemplated going after him, just to keep him from bothering their guest. That ploy, she decided, would probably not fool anyone. She heard Lauren talking to him, followed by her throaty laughter, and caught just a glimpse of a white thigh and hip as Lauren went to open the closet. Maris hurried to the kitchen and took a beer from the refrigerator.

Darkness had fallen when Lauren finally emerged, wearing beige Dockers and an emerald-green long-sleeved blouse. She was strikingly beautiful. Smiling at Maris, she said, "Where are you taking me?"

Swallowing the last of her beer, Maris replied, "Anywhere you want to go. What are you hungry for?"

"I haven't had good Mexican food and a margarita since I got back to Texas."

"It's a pretty night. Should we take the 'vertible?"

"I was hoping that we would." Lauren smiled, holding up an elastic band. She pulled her hair back and skillfully wrapped the band around it, forming a ponytail.

Leaving Earnhardt in the backyard, they quickly climbed into the convertible. The weather was perfect for riding with the top down — not too warm, but chilly enough to feel exhilarating. With the light Monday evening traffic, they were in Dallas within thirty minutes. Maris chose a small restaurant on Maple, not far from the Crossroads, the gay section of Dallas. They found parking near the front door. Lauren released her ponytail, and they both hastily brushed their hair. Maris decided to raise the top on the convertible and was relieved when the electrical motor worked flawlessly.

The small Mexican restaurant was doing a brisk Monday evening business. A waiter showed them a quiet corner table and took their drink orders. Maris ordered margaritas, and another waiter delivered water, chips and hot sauce to their table. Soft Mexican music played in the background.

"This is very nice," Lauren said as the green margaritas arrived. She licked a bit of salt off the rim and took a sip. "Very good." She sighed.

"I'm glad you like it. Have you been to this part of Dallas before?"

"The Crossroads? Once, in college. With my first ex." She leaned across the table and added, "A high school basketball coach attending summer school."

"Where would we be without those coaches?" Maris laughed.

"Was your first a coach?"

"No, my first was a bitch." Maris grinned. The waiter reappeared and took their orders. Both wanted cheese enchiladas with the usual rice and beans.

"So where did you get your name? It's unusual." Lauren dipped a chip in the hot sauce and took a bite.

"My father was an avid baseball fan, and of course he expected a boy. When I surprised him by being a girl, he decided that he couldn't call me Roger or Mickey as he planned, so he went with the last names, Maris and Mantle. And I'm Maris Mantle Middleton — at least Yogi Berra wasn't his favorite player."

"My father didn't follow sports."

"My sister also got an interesting name from Dad, Landry Middleton. Everyone calls her Lana. She is the real jock in the family; makes me look like a little thing. She almost made an Olympic volleyball team, but tore up her knee. Now she's an assistant coach at UT. The surprising thing is that she is straight as a fucking arrow — and married."

"Does your family know about you?"

"Mary Ann and I'd been together about three years when they figured it out. It was hard for them, but they accepted it. They loved her. My parents live in Sweetwater, just west of Abilene. Since I opened the lab, I haven't spent the time with them I should."

"You're lucky to have an accepting family."

Their meal arrived, and they ate hungrily, making mostly small talk about current affairs, the FBI and DPS. When they were finished, the waiter discreetly set the check on the end of the table. Maris reached for it, but Lauren lightly squeezed her wrist, sending an electrical current up her arm. "Let me," she said softly. "I invited you out, remember? And, you're letting me stay with you."

"Earnhardt and I are happy to have you there. Believe me, you've brightened our dull household. I'll let you get it, if you'll let me take you out for a drink, and a little dancing?"

"Dancing?" Lauren said, retrieving the check. "What kind of dancing?"

"You'll see. Shall we go?"

Maris was glad that the top was up on the convertible since the fall night air had turned cooler. They drove a few blocks from the restaurant and stopped at a small bar not far from a tangled crisscross of overpasses near downtown Dallas. Brightly lit tall towers outlining the skyline could be seen intermittently between the raised highways and billboards. There were several cars in the parking lot, more than Maris expected for a Monday night.

Maris stopped at the bar to buy beer while Lauren found a table not far away where Maris could see Monday Night Football on the big-screen TV and the action on the dance floor. The sound on the TV was muted and the d.j. played a pleasant mix of country and rock music. The women at the bar glanced at Maris and did a double take at Lauren before returning reluctantly to the football game. Another group of women celebrated a birthday at a large corner table and kept the dance floor busy.

Maris set the longneck beer bottles on the table and looked down at Lauren as a good country two-step started playing. "You asked what kind of dancing? How about this?" she asked, extending her hand.

"Hey, girl, I was born in Fredericksburg, Texas, German country, and lived there until I was fifteen. I can do it all."

Lauren grasped Maris's hand and pulled her onto the dance floor. There were some appreciative glances from the other women as they watched Lauren. Maris took her into her arms surprised at how easily she followed her. Lauren smiled at her as she led them through a series of spins. Her touch was light, but electrifying, on Maris's neck and shoulder. It had been much too long since she danced with a beautiful woman. They danced through several songs before stopping breathlessly to drink their beers that were already rodeo cool.

"You're beautiful," Maris said, pulling her chair closer to Lauren's. "And you're a good dancer. How the hell did an O'Conner end up in German country?"

"Thank you, you're not a bad dancer yourself. I'm German-Irish, so be careful," Lauren said, smiling at Maris. Maris leaned toward her and kissed her lightly on the lips, waiting for her to push her away or murmur a protest. When neither happened, Maris became bolder and pressed her lips tighter against Lauren's, parting them slightly. She pulled back and touched Lauren's hair as one of Maris's favorite country songs, a classic Ray Price, started playing.

"Now that's beer-drinking, honky-tonk music. Shall we?" Maris drained the last of her beer and they joined the women from the birthday party on the dance floor.

Lauren's arm was around her neck as they moved to the fast-paced two-step. The next song was a George Strait waltz, and she pulled Lauren closer to her, well aware of her full breasts as they brushed against her. They complemented each other well on the dance floor, with only a few miscues as Lauren followed Maris's lead effortlessly through a series of turns and twirls.

Hot and thirsty, they returned to the table and Maris said, "One more beer before we go?" Lauren nodded, and Maris went to the bar.

When she returned, Lauren leaned over and said, "Coming here was a good idea." They drank in silence, watching the birthday party grow and get louder. A baby butch was turning the ripe old age of twenty-two. "Remember being that young?" Lauren asked.

"Some of it, but I like being in my thirties. Just think of all the things we know that they're just beginning to learn."

"But not all that we know is good, or happy."

"No, but it's life."

"And those who survive are made stronger and wiser?"

"That's what I keep telling myself."

"Take me home, Maris Mantle Middleton. I'm suddenly very tired."

They drove home in silence, listening to the radio. Lauren's arm rested lightly on the seat near Maris, and Maris stole a glance at her, shifting into fourth gear as they entered the highway. Lauren rested her head back on the seat and rode with her eyes closed, but Maris could feel her fingers drumming on the seat and sometimes brushing her shoulder in time to the music. What are we fixing to get into, she wondered as she drove faster and felt a chill of anticipation. The traffic was light, and they were in Allen within twenty-five minutes.

Maris unlocked the door leading into the kitchen and Lauren swept closely past her. Maris turned on the lights and deactivated the alarm while Lauren opened the back door and let a joyous Earnhardt inside. He leaned against Maris's leg, and she stroked him distractedly before moving toward Lauren. She stopped close behind her, and Lauren turned. Maris embraced her fully, kissing her firmly on the lips. She felt Lauren's breath catch before she accepted Maris's tongue. She finished her kiss and lightly brushed Lauren's soft hair, inhaling the remnants of her perfume mixed with sweat and cigarette smoke. It was intoxicatingly sexy.

She caressed Lauren's cheek and kissed her again, much more gently and less urgently. She felt Lauren's hands run through her hair and lock around her neck. Smiling and looking into Lauren's eyes, Maris unbuttoned Lauren's top button, then the second, and the third until she had completely opened her blouse. She reached underneath, encircling her waist, marveling at the feel of the smooth, bare skin. She continued to kiss her, and her hands moved to the clasps on her bra. Out of practice, she struggled momentarily but was rewarded when Lauren's breasts sprang free. The nipple responded instantly to her touch. Maris felt Lauren's fingers on the buttons to her shirt. She released Lauren's breast and stepped away, taking Lauren by the hand.

"Come on," she whispered, pulling Lauren to her bedroom. She kissed Lauren and pushed her gently down on the bed. She reached back and opened the upper curtain on the window, allowing a stream of moonlight and the glow of an outside security light to penetrate the dark room. She saw Lauren smiling up at her and resisted the urge to rip off her shirt and jeans, forcing herself to move slowly, aware that Lauren followed every move.

She went to Lauren, kissing her neck and lips as she reached down, unbuckled Lauren's belt and unbuttoned her Dockers. She tossed the pants over the side of the bed and heard Earnhardt sigh disgustedly, get up and move to another spot on the floor.

They laughed and looked at each other with the

embarrassment of new lovers. Maris murmured, "You're beautiful," and they resumed. She stroked Lauren's panties and was amused at the dampness she found. She caressed the inside of Lauren's thighs, pushing her legs apart. She stroked the soft pubic hair before gliding a finger inside. Lauren raised her hips and pressed against her. Refusing to be hurried, Maris forced a second finger in and explored gently before withdrawing. Lauren took her panties off and reached out to touch Maris's breast. Maris slipped two fingers inside, increasing the rhythm as Lauren pumped her hips. Leaving a trail of kisses down Lauren's stomach, Maris slid downward and inhaled the feminine aroma. She lowered her head.

Lauren gasped, and her back arched. Soon, Lauren's legs tensed, and she came with a loud groan and a rush of air forced through clenched teeth.

Slowly, Maris removed her fingers and pushed herself onto one elbow. She reached for the top sheet and wiped her face before sliding up beside Lauren. Maris stretched her neck to one side and heard it pop. Lauren laughed, breathlessly, and muttered under Maris's kiss, "Did I break it?"

Maris laughed stroking Lauren's hair. She could see a flash of red under the soft light from the window. Lauren rolled toward her and kissed her. She found Maris's breast and then reached between Maris's legs. Maris shuddered, already excited. She fleetingly thought of Mary Ann but felt no guilt, which both surprised and relieved her. She realized that her memories of Mary Ann had become pleasant and sweet, no longer sad and anguished. Her body, long denied, reacted quickly and strongly to Lauren.

"Maris?" Lauren said a few moments later, her

back against Maris's stomach and chest. "This is my kind of sports."

Maris laughed softly and soon fell asleep, holding Lauren.

Chapter Five

Maris sat up sleepily and looked at the clock. It was only five, and the other side of the bed was empty. She dressed quickly in shorts and a T-shirt, then went into the living room and found Lauren sitting on the couch wearing a full-length silky maroon housecoat. Her feet were curled up under her and she sipped a cup of coffee. Earnhardt slept on the floor nearby.

"You're up early," Maris said as she sat down.

"Ghosts always come at dawn for me. What about you?"

"I think my ghosts are all at rest."

Lauren turned toward Maris, and she accepted the invitation for a kiss. "Thank you for last night," Lauren said. "It was wonderful!"

"I think that's what I'm supposed to say."

"Come with me today. I don't want to go back there alone."

"Lauren, I'm not trained to interrogate witnesses, but you are. You don't need me."

"Yes, I do. I have to talk to the Chief and more of Karin's friends, and I have to do a background check on Bennie."

"I don't think you'll have to dig very deep to find something on him. Why don't you get the Texas Rangers involved?"

"I think somebody's already involved, but I don't know what he's found out. He may not have really done anything yet. I don't know. Please come with me?"

"I wish I could, but I've got to work the drug cases that were dropped off yesterday while we were gone. I usually do blood alcohols on Tuesday, and I don't have any fancy automated systems to do it for me. Then, there's your evidence, and I have to pick up the pictures from yesterday. I'm sorry. A fast turnaround is the only way I can compete with the government labs."

"I know, and your business is still new. I didn't mean to put pressure on you." She smiled, tossing back her red hair. "So, the least you can do is make love to me one more time, if you won't go with me."

"I thought you were going to ask me to do something difficult," Maris said, pulling the belt loose on Lauren's housecoat. "What do you have on under here?"

This time, they made love urgently, passionately, more hungrily than the first time. They soon moved from the sofa to the floor, much to Earnhardt's disgust.

Afterwards, they lay quietly on the floor, shivering in the cool morning air and hugging each other tightly. It was light outside when Maris stood up and helped Lauren to her feet. "To the showers," Maris said. "Care to join me?"

"Not this time." She laughed. "I swear I'm sore already. I think I'll just use the back shower, by myself."

Maris laughed too as she picked up her clothes. "By the way, before I forget, your house key is on the bar in the kitchen."

Maris was already working in the lab when Lauren came in to give her a passionate good-bye kiss. "Blood, yuck," she said, looking down at the vacutainers of blood lined up on the workbench.

"What kind of FBI agent are you that you let a little blood bother you?" Maris teased.

"A soon-to-be-broke FBI agent if I don't find some answers soon and get back to work."

Maris felt her stomach knot up. She hadn't stopped to think that Lauren was only in Texas temporarily.

Lauren's smile faded. "Karin stayed with me for

almost two months after Irene divorced her first husband. She was only five then. Children are so much fun at that age. She visited me for two weeks every summer until two years ago. Seems like after that neither of us had time."

"Sounds like Karin's lucky to have an aunt like you."

"I don't know. The last day of her visit was always traumatic. She cried and begged to stay with me. I thought it was because I spoiled her. Now I wonder — was it because Bobby Joe was abusing her?"

Somewhat down after she left, Maris finished setting up the blood samples for alcohol determination before pausing to check the blood from Karin's blouse. The results surprised her. The sample tested positive for goat blood. Instantly, her mind flashed to the articles she'd read about Satanism. Supposedly, goats were sacrificed as part of the devil-worshiping rituals, and sometimes the participants drank the blood. What was Lauren's niece involved in, she wondered, and was it voluntary? She tried to call Lauren on her mobile phone but received no answer.

The blood-alcohol analysis went quickly and smoothly. She finished in less than three hours, cleaned up afterwards and sealed the blood vacutainers back into their original packaging. The telephone rang before she could complete the paperwork. It was Lauren.

"Something's happened. A girl in foster care with Brian Blake's parents has accused them of molestation, sexual abuse and devil worship. Supposedly, Brian's also involved. The girl — she's only ten — told a teacher last Friday that she dreaded the weekend. When the teacher asked why, the girl became distraught, and the teacher took her to the nurse's office. She told them a horrifying story, and they called in the police and child welfare. Since the Blakes live outside city limits, the sheriff's office was involved, and they brought in a Texas Ranger, Wayne Coffey.

"I know Wayne. He's good, and he'll investigate thoroughly. Does he know about the connection between Brian and Karin?"

"Yes, they talked to the girl off and on all the weekend and most of yesterday. Some, but not all, of the experts seem to believe her. Child welfare knows that she was sexually assaulted by her father, with her mother's consent, before she was taken away and placed in foster care. She had also made an accusation against her last foster family, saying that the foster father had molested her, so her credibility is at stake. The authorities are sure that it was false. That family had been involved in foster care for years with no other problems, and the man passed a polygraph. Now she claims that her new foster parents, some of their relatives and Brian are all involved in Satanism and bizarre sexual rituals. She says that a pretty blond girl —" Lauren's voice broke momentarily before she drew a deep breath and continued. "A blond girl was held captive for several days in a back bedroom of the house. She saw her naked in handcuffs. She says that she saw different men have sex with this girl over a period of several days."

"Jesus Christ," Maris said.

"God, if it's true, what she must have gone through."

58

"Don't think about that. What's Wayne doing now?"

"They're not sure if they have enough for a search warrant yet, due to the false accusations against the last foster family. They've decided to pick Brian up and bring him in for questioning. See what they can get out of him and proceed from there."

"I may have some information for Wayne," Maris said. "This morning, after you left, I read the results of tests on the blood from the Karin's blouse. It appears to be goat blood."

"Goat blood?"

"Yeah, Satanic cults often sacrifice goats and may even drink the blood as part of their rituals."

"Oh, my God!" Lauren exclaimed. "Oh, Maris, what was Karin involved with, and where is she now?" She paused. "Please come to Pierce."

"I don't know, Lauren. If Wayne is investigating, he'll use the DPS lab, not me, and he may not appreciate my presence."

"I'll work it out. He's agreed, since I'm FBI, to let me observe any interrogations and tag along on the search warrant when we get it. I already told him about the allegations against Bennie. He didn't seem surprised."

"With Wayne, you wouldn't know if he was surprised or not. Why don't you wait until they question Brian? See what happens there and call me. If they get a search warrant and Wayne agrees, I'll come down. I want to be with you, Lauren. I've missed you all morning, but this is too important for us to risk alienating anyone or interfering with the outcome."

Maris was alarmed by the silence on the other

end, but finally Lauren sighed. "I understand, Maris. It's just that I'm afraid of what we may find. I want to know the truth, but at the same time I dread the knowledge. Do you understand?"

"Yes, I understand," she said, quietly. What was wrong with her? How could she even consider letting Lauren down? "I'll be there in about two hours, and I'll bring my supplies, camera and everything, just in case."

There was a sigh of relief on the other end of the line. "Thank you."

Chapter Six

It was almost one-thirty when Maris found Lauren waiting in the tiny coffee room of the Sheriff's Department in Pierce. "Hello, beautiful," she whispered. "How're you doing?"

"Better, now." She smiled. "We're waiting for Brian's lawyer to arrive so that we can continue the interrogation, if he lets us. God, Maris, he's awful. I can't imagine the Karin that I know having anything to do with him."

Maris bought a soft drink and talked with the other officers. She was strongly aware of Lauren's presence and wondered how anyone could be oblivious to her feelings. She was thinking she should go outside and take a short walk when Texas Ranger Wayne Coffey stuck his head into the room.

"Oh, hi, Maris, how've you been?" he asked, stepping into the room to shake her hand. He was, indeed, impressive. Almost a full six feet five inches tall, he wore the usual Ranger uniform, a white Western shirt, Western-cut trousers, boots and a wide-brimmed white straw cowboy hat. It had not been cold enough yet to switch to winter felt. "I've missed you at the lab. Understand you have your own now. Hope it works out for you."

"Thanks, Wayne," Maris said. He had long been her favorite Ranger.

"His shyster is here, and he's agreed that we can talk to the little weasel as long as he's present. We're ready to start, if you want to follow the Chief into the adjoining room. You can see through the two-way mirror, and we'll have the sound on in there."

"Thank you." Lauren smiled at him, and Maris realized that she was probably not the only one in the room smitten by the pretty redhead. She greeted Chief Wilkes in the hallway and they went to the interrogation room. She immediately saw what Lauren was talking about. Brian Blake was a tall, gangly, pimply-faced youth who sported pierced ears and numerous tattoos. Maris was disgusted. On his right forearm was a fiery goat's head, and on his biceps he wore the numbers *666*. His other arm had an inverted cross and an upside down pentagram. As she watched, he gripped the sides of his straight-backed chair and angled it away from the table a few inches.

Leaning toward Lauren, she whispered, "Jesus, no wonder you were surprised to see him. Note the tattoos."

"He's awful. Look at his pierced nose."

Wayne Coffey led the interrogation, and Chief Deputy Ralph Lambert assisted him. They had purposely excluded Bennie Wright, who was out on patrol. Maris was pleased to see Ralph Lambert. About Maris's age, he had started work at the Sheriff's Office about the same time Maris started with the DPS lab. While still a rookie deputy, he busted the son of a prominent Dallas attorney with two hundred pounds of marijuana. The case generated a lot of publicity in Dallas and Pierce. The attorney, assisting in his son's defense, smelled blood when he found out he had a rookie cop and a rookie chemist on the case. He tried every dirty trick in the book. Ralph was on the stand for three grueling days and Maris for two. But the jury didn't buy the defense team's shenanigans and gave the boy twenty-five years. Over the last ten years, they'd worked together on many cases and Maris had watched him move up the ladder until he made Chief Deputy. Rumors were, ol' Sheriff Sizemore was within two years of retirement and wanted Ralph to replace him. Maris wished that the S.O. had been in charge of Karin's case from the beginning.

Standing across the table from Brian, the Ranger asked, "You involved in devil worship, Brian?"

"So what if I am. It's not against the law." He leaned back in his chair, stretched his legs out and crossed his arms over his chest.

"No, it's not against the law. Not unless you're doing something besides just worshiping. You wouldn't know anything about some sacrifices, would you?"

"Of course not. That would be against the law, wouldn't it."

"How many people are in your little group? Your parents worship the devil?"

"Yes, but we obey the law."

"What about your foster sister, Cindy?"

"What about her?"

"She says that your daddy and you had sexual intercourse with her. What do you say about that?"

Straightening in his chair, he said, "That's ridiculous! She's a little girl. I like women, not children. So does my Dad."

"What about your girlfriend, Karin Beauchamp?" the Ranger asked Brian.

Maris was surprised to see the insolent young man look momentarily grief-stricken, but he caught himself and recovered. "I don't know anything about where she is."

"Did you see her that Friday night after the football game?"

"Yeah. Me, Jack Trevor and Gene Simmons met her and Heather and Jennifer out at Devil's Leg after the game."

"I can't believe that there's really a place by that name around here," Lauren whispered.

"Coincidence, I'll tell you about it later," Maris replied.

"We smoked some dope and fooled around a little bit. Then the girls had to leave. They had to drop Karin off to meet her old man, and Jennifer and Heather had to be home by twelve o'clock."

Maris noticed that the deputy had picked up a

telephone in the corner of the room and was speaking into it.

"I don't understand," Brian whined. "I've answered all of these questions for the police. I don't know what happened to her."

"Your foster sister says that Karin was held captive at your house and that you and several other men raped her. This part of your devil-worshiping group, a little ritual that you practice?"

"That's bullshit! I loved Karin, and I wouldn't let anything like that happen to her."

"We have information that she crawled out of her window to meet someone. Was that someone you?"

"No."

Wayne pulled a chair away from the table and propped his foot in the seat. He placed an arm across his knee and leaned forward, towering over the table. "I don't believe you. Even your parents say that you came home very late that Friday night, or more accurately, early Saturday morning. Where were you?"

"I was just out fooling around."

"Didn't you pick her up a few yards from her house and take her to your home where she was abused sexually by the men in your cult?"

"No, absolutely not!"

"A blouse was found in Karin's room that was bloody. Do you know anything about that?"

"Fuck, no!"

"The blood was goat blood. Don't you people use goat blood in your ceremonies?"

"No!" Brian sat rigid in his chair, glaring at Wayne.

"Did you take Karin to one of those rituals and use goat blood? Did you make her drink it?"

"I don't know what you're talking about."

"Ranger Coffey, he's already answered those questions and said that he doesn't know anything about Karin's disappearance. I don't think he needs to answer any more questions about that subject," the lawyer, James Bradley, interjected.

"Well, Mr. Bradley, we have a witness that has come forward this morning, after we went to school to pick up Brian," Wayne said. "Tell him what information we have." He nodded to Deputy Lambert.

"A female student, friend of yours, says that she has taken part in several of your cult meetings, rituals, whatever you want to call them. She's seen you at these meetings with Karin Beauchamp. She claims that, as part of a special initiation rite, a goat was slaughtered and Karin was made to drink the goat blood with the rest of the worshipers," the deputy explained.

"What about that, Brian?"

"You don't have to answer if you don't want to, Brian," the lawyer said. "We can stop this at least until you and I talk."

"The Sheriff's office has had a busy morning," Lauren said dryly as the Ranger paused in his questioning to allow Brian to ponder his predicament. "Why didn't the police department have any of this information?"

The Chief shrugged. "I don't know. Maybe these kids were afraid to talk until they thought that Brian had been arrested."

Maybe, Maris thought, or your boy, Bennie, didn't want all of this to come out.

"What about it, Brian? Was she there? What did you do next? This is looking bad for you, boy. We have another friend of yours who claims that he loaned you his car the night that Karin disappeared, because your car wasn't running. Do you think we'll find anything inside it? If you didn't kill her, you better quit lying and tell us the truth. Gene Simmons has agreed to let the crime lab examine his car," the Ranger said. "Come on, Brian. Tell us what happened. Sex get a little too rough, go a little too far? It was an accident, right?"

James Bradley said, "Wayne —"

Suddenly Brian's face contorted in fury and his voice rapidly deepened as he screamed, "The goat's head breathes fire and blood! Let him who has understanding reckon the number of the beast. Its number is six hundred and sixty-six. Mine is the Kingdom of Darkness. We are washed not in the blood of the lamb, but the blood of the goat. I mark you forever as an enemy of the beast." He spit into the Ranger's face.

"You little son-of-a-bitch!" Ranger Coffey swore as he kicked the chair away from the table. "I'll teach you about the King of Darkness." He reached for Brian as Ralph sprang in between them. Brian was laughing crazily.

Restraining his client, the lawyer hissed, "Shut up, Brian, you fool! Don't say another word. Jesus!"

"You little bastard, I'm charging you with assault on a peace officer, and you can just cool your little ass in jail while we sort through this mess. Get him the fuck out of here. Book him on the new charges," the Ranger said as he wiped his face off with his handkerchief.

"God damn," Maris said. "It's a wonder Wayne didn't pound the little bastard into the ground."

"This may be a break for us. Now we can hold him on the new charges," Lauren said.

"God, Wayne," the lawyer said, apologetically. "I didn't know he was such a crazy bastard."

"You better warn that little fucker that stunts like that won't help him any. If he's trying to build an insanity defense, it won't work."

After Wayne Coffey regained his composure, they gathered in the Sheriff's conference room.

"You heard the interrogation, what do you think?" the Ranger asked, looking at Lauren.

"He knows something. I think his stunt was a method to avoid further questioning."

"Possibly. I think that he's been getting Karin more and more involved in this Satan-worshiping, and they met the Friday she disappeared. Maybe the ritual went too far and she was killed. Maybe the foster sister is telling the truth and she was held for a few days. She could be dead, or she could still be in captivity somewhere."

"Oh, God, that would be terrible," Lauren said.

"What about the witness you were talking about?" Maris asked.

Ralph said, "Shortly after we left the school with Brian, a girl named Elaine Johnson called and asked if he'd been arrested. The call was transferred to the Sheriff since we knew it might be important. He persuaded her to let us send a car and bring her in to talk to us. When she arrived, we told her that Brian Blake was a suspect in the disappearance and possible homicide of Karin Beauchamp. I implied that if she withheld information she could be charged. The Sheriff is with her now, but what I've been told is fantastic." He paused and looked around the room briefly before he continued. "It's scary, I have a daughter ..." He shook his head. "Elaine says that there's a group of Satan-worshipers at the school and that several adults are involved. She says that the teenage boys are supposed to recruit new members, particularly young girls. The initiation rites involve drinking goat blood and having sex with each cult member. She claims that Brian's cult is a small one in a whole secret society of other small cults and only the adult leaders know who's involved in the entire society. This is for security, she claims. Apparently, some community leaders are involved. I'm not sure I believe all of her story."

"FBI investigations in the past have always found that the stories about widespread Satanic cults were overblown. The last investigation concluded that only a few unorganized but sick individuals were involved," Lauren said.

"We hear a lot of stories, but we've never been able to really substantiate an elaborate organization. Some people say that we're unsuccessful because of the extreme secrecy of the groups and the way they allow only a few leaders to know the full extent of the organization. I don't know what to think," Wayne said.

"What does Elaine say about Karin specifically?" Maris asked.

"She's still being questioned, but she says that Karin is a recent recruit. On the Friday she disappeared, Brian picked her up about twelve-thirty or one a.m. and took her out to where they have their meetings. We're going out there as soon as we execute the search warrant on the Blake residence. We'll get the warrants when we conclude here. With the help of Child Welfare, the Sheriff convinced the judge that we couldn't wait to go out there, especially after Brian admitted to involvement in the devil worship."

"So, Brian picked Karin up. Did she make it to the meeting?"

"Apparently. And they performed one of their usual rituals which culminated with a sexual orgy, according to Elaine. Then Brian left to take Karin home in Gene Simmons's car."

Wayne said, "We've impounded the car, and it'll be examined by the DPS crime lab. You and Maris are welcome to come with us on the search — they hold their cere- monies in a field — and the search on the Blake residence, if you want. DPS lab is sending a team out to help us." He glanced at Lauren.

"Thanks. If this is big enough, the FBI may be interested anyway."

"There's one more piece of information that Elaine's given us," Ralph said. "She says that one of the adults has taken a special interest in Karin and that Brian was getting jealous. This adult didn't attend the meeting that night, and Karin seemed upset. While the others were engaged in various sexual acts, Karin and Brian argued. Elaine said that some of the other males talked to Karin and were angry that she rejected Brian. Sex is supposed to be part of belonging to the cult. Elaine claims that the adult participant, who was missing that night, is your officer, Chief. Name's Bennie Wright."

"I can't imagine him being involved in any of this," Chief Wilkes said, shaking his head. "He goes to church regularly, coaches Little League."

"At this point, we're still in the investigative

stage. We don't know if it's true or not, but it might be a good idea to put him on administrative leave," Ranger Coffey said.

"I'll bring him in on desk duty immediately."

"Chief, you should know that I have statements from other kids who claim that Bennie and Karin may have had something going," Lauren said.

"Make those statements available to me and my department will investigate. I have to say that I'll be very disappointed if any of this turns out to be true."

"I think we all agree that it's always disappointing when a policeman is involved in something he shouldn't be," the Ranger said. "We'll have the search warrant soon. I'll let you know when we get it."

Chief Wilkes stood and said, "Wayne, I don't think I'll go with you. Keep me informed. It seems that I have a little internal investigation of my own to perform."

Maris handed the Ranger a piece of paper with her beeper number written on it. "We'll be in town. Please beep me when you're ready to go, and we'll be here within ten minutes. Put in six-six-six, and I'll know who it is and what you want."

"Very funny, Maris." Wayne laughed. "But, for you and the FBI, anything."

Chapter Seven

The warmth of the unusually hot September sun struck Maris as she and Lauren stepped outside. She couldn't remember a drier September in recent years. Lauren, interrupting her thoughts, asked, "Now what?"

"Since we have time to kill, I want to go out to Devil's Leg Crossing."

"Looking for something specific?"

"No, not really, but I think I'll feel like we're overlooking something if we don't at least go look."

"You know where it is?"

"Sure, Mary Ann and I went canoeing there several years ago. Let me tell you about Devil's Leg Crossing," Maris said as Lauren walked beside her to the Ford pickup. "It's a low-water crossing on a small tributary off the Sabine River. Shaped like a dog's hind leg, it was originally called Dog's Leg Crossing. Early settlers crossed the river there in buggies and wagons. The water on each side is deep with good fishing, but the actual crossing is shallow." Riding with the windows down on the truck, Maris watched for the county road, only a couple of miles from town, that led to Devil's Leg Crossing. "When they first discovered oil in East Texas, back in the twenties, men poured in by the dozens from all over the country to get jobs as roughnecks. Pierce grew rapidly and problems developed with gambling, prostitution, illegal stills and so forth. There was a killing almost every day and naturally, the decent citizens complained. Finally, the Governor ordered a Texas Ranger to Pierce to handle the problem."

Lauren laughed and said, "Don't tell me, 'One riot, one Ranger.' "

"Now listen, that's another story. The Ranger, outnumbered, solicited the Sheriff's help. Together, they arrested twenty-five of the worst men in town. They closed the saloons and the whorehouses, and the Ranger told the town in a meeting on the square, 'I've come to take the devil by the leg and throw him out of this town, by any means necessary.' The townspeople quickly convened a court and found five of the men guilty of murder and sentenced them to hang. The Ranger took the five men out to the clearing near Dog's Leg Crossing and placed the nooses on the branches of a massive oak tree."

73

Maris stopped on the shoulder of the two-lane county road across from a small park complete with picnic tables, grills and trash barrels. Judging by the graffiti-covered tables and beer cans and bottles scattered everywhere, it seemed that kids had taken over the area. A towering oak tree, surrounded by a wrought iron fence with a tarnished plaque, stood majestically to one side. Reaching out with strong twisted limbs, the oak formed a protective canopy over a nearby concrete picnic table.

"There's the tree. Shame this place is trashed out now," Maris said. "They brought the sentenced men to this tree to hang, but some of their friends tried to stop the hanging and rescue the convicts. A shoot-out ensued, and after killing many men, the Ranger was finally gunned down. The townspeople intervened and drove off the remaining outlaws before they could save their buddies. The five men were hanged. They said that the river ran red with blood that day making it look like the devil's leg. Others said that the name came from the Ranger's promise to 'throw the devil out by the leg.' Either way, the name stuck. According to legend, this place is haunted, which makes it a favorite hangout for the kids."

Covering ground deeply rutted by heavy vehicular traffic, they walked to the crossing. Although the river was muddy on each side, the gravel bottom of the shallow area, alive with darting minnows and small shad, was clearly visible. Old broken reels and empty worm boxes littered the banks of the river near a narrow trail on both sides of the crossing.

Following the trail around a sharp turn, they discovered a clearing with the remnants of a bonfire near the center. The strong odor of decay assaulted them, freezing them.

"Oh, God," Lauren said, breaking the silence as her hand flew to cover her mouth.

"Wait here and let me look around. It could be from a dead animal," Maris said, dreading what she might find as she stepped into the clearing. Blackened, brittle bones mixed with the cold ashes of the campfire. A large willow tree near the riverbank was marred with deeply engraved inverted crosses and a crude goat's head. Following the odor, Maris approached the river. Without warning, her right foot plunged into the soft ground and she fell forward, catching herself with her hands. She scrambled up instantly.

Lauren came to her, ashen-faced, and asked in a strained voice, "It's not a grave?"

"Maybe," Maris said, walking around briefly to ease the pain in her ankle. She knelt down in the loose dirt. "It's too small for a human grave." She shoveled the soil with her hands until gray fur was visible. Using a stick, she removed more dirt and saw a cloven hoof. "I think it's a goat."

She stopped digging and they returned to her pickup to retrieve the camera, gloves, shovel, evidence tags, trash bags and envelopes. After taking photographs of the clearing, the carvings on the tree and the partially exposed grave, Maris quickly excavated the goat. She finally uncovered the last of it and exclaimed, "Its head is gone!"

"This is sick," Lauren said, bending to help Maris put the badly decaying body into a trash bag.

"Let's save it to show Ralph and Wayne. The smaller bones by the campfire appear to be animal, but we'll take them to the sheriff's office. They can have an expert check them to make sure." Maris snapped off her gloves and wrinkled her nose. The goat stank.

"If nothing else, it seems to reinforce this Satanism thing. Ralph is going to love us for bringing this stinky goat back to the S.O."

Returning to town, they stopped in the convenience store, used the restroom to clean up and bought something cold to drink. As Maris paid for the Cokes, she said, "I suppose that this is where Karin met her stepfather."

Lauren nodded and pointed to a flyer with Karin's photograph taped to the cash register.

"You're talking about the missing girl?" the elderly male cashier said. "I was working the night she disappeared. I wonder where that child could be. I'm afraid that I fear the worst for her." His voice trailed as he handed Maris the change.

"I suppose you saw her get into the pickup with her stepfather, Bobby Joe?" Lauren asked.

"Yes, I remember that night because Karin, I didn't know her name then, but I'd seen her around. Anyway, I remember because she came to the store with Officer Wright. I was afraid she was in trouble with the law, or something. In my day, pretty young ladies didn't get into trouble like that. Then, the father, or stepfather, showed up and had an argument with Officer Wright."

"Did you say that she came to the store in the officer's police car?" Maris asked, sipping her Coke.

"Yep, I asked him about the argument later when he came in for a cup of coffee. Seems the girl had been stranded by friends and he gave her a lift so she could ride home with her father. The father had been drinking, and Officer Wright wanted the girl to drive. I guess the dad resented it."

Lauren and Maris exchanged glances and turned to leave.

The cashier added, "Officer Wright was still here when we saw the Dodge truck drive by again. I thought there'd be trouble for sure. I just hoped that he didn't have a wreck before the officer could stop him. I even wondered if he was looking for the officer to start something. Officer Wright said that everything would be fine, not to worry, and he left to go after the Dodge."

Lauren instantly returned to the counter. "You saw the same pickup later that same night?"

"Yeah, that truck is easy to recognize. There aren't many Dodge trucks in town like it, and none of the others are dual rear-wheeled."

"What time would you say that you saw the truck the second time?" Lauren asked. She was writing everything in her small notebook.

"Probably sometime around one-thirty or two o'clock that morning."

"Could you see who was in the truck?"

"No, just a glimpse of the truck as it passed by the store. Are you a lady cop?"

Lauren smiled. "Actually, I'm FBI, but I'm on a leave of absence. Karin is my niece, and I appreciate your help. One more question — when did you see Officer Wright again?"

"He came in for coffee about four-thirty or five

that morning. We go off duty at about seven, and he often comes by for coffee and breakfast before he goes home to sleep."

Lauren wrote down the cashier's name, address and phone number. Maris's beeper went off and she read the numbers *666*. They rushed to the Sheriff's Department.

Chapter Eight

The search of the Blake residence was a waste of time, Maris thought, as she and Lauren walked through the old farmhouse. Like any home with lots of kids and a low income, the house and furnishings were tired and worn, although the kitchen and bathrooms were clean and neat. She'd imagined the back bedroom with wall-mounted restraints and blood-spattered walls, but it seemed rather innocuous with a double bed and one bureau in the corner. The bed had a white bedspread, not the color Maris would imagine in a room of torture.

She and Lauren watched as the officers searched the barn and a storage shed without uncovering anything suspicious.

Wayne joined them and said, "They haven't found anything. I'm going to have the DPS lab Luminol the inside of the shed and the back bedroom. If they don't find anything, I may get the deputies to rip up the shed floor. Ralph will stay with them. We better get over to the clearing before it gets dark."

With only two hours till dusk, Maris and Lauren followed Wayne and two deputies to the site of the alleged Satanic ceremonies. Screened from the county road by wild scrub oak and tall sunflowers, the clearing was difficult to find. Scattered wild pecans, pines and oak trees also shrouded the clearing from the eyes of a casual passerby.

The Ranger drove slowly until he reached a makeshift gate where the barbed wire and a couple of posts had been cut and propped back into place. Leaving the vehicles by the side of the road, Ranger Coffey, Lauren, Maris and the two deputies followed the rutted dirt path for several dozen yards before they emerged in a clearing about one hundred feet in diameter. An old farmhouse once stood on the site, but all that remained was one corner of a crumbling natural stone wall and a portion of the fireplace hearth. A large wooden box, the size of an army footlocker and secured with a padlock, was chained to a metal ring drilled into the surviving fireplace wall. Dried red stains were visible on the front stones. The sparse grass in the clearing was bent and worn from heavy vehicular and foot traffic.

Ashes from an old fire blackened the center of the clearing in a pit marked off by several large rocks.

Beer cans and bottles were scattered around. Some labels looked new, but others were torn, cracked and weathered. Numerous cigarette butts were present. Maris spotted the top ring of a condom with the rest of the latex torn away.

"Looks like a good place to have a beer bust, if you're underage," Maris said.

"I suppose we better open that box," the Ranger said, pointing to the fireplace.

Maris retrieved her pickup and drove it into the clearing. Taking her hammer and a pair of gloves from the truck, Maris prepared to open the lock using a trick a narcotics agent once taught her. She rapped the lock in the right place with the hammer, and it sprang open. She knelt and flipped up the lid to the box. The pungent odor of rotten meat filled the air.

"God damn," Maris said as a horde of flies and other insects rose from the box. She saw the eyes first, several pairs of dead, staring, glassy eyes from a pile of animal heads. A gray goat's head was the largest and freshest in the box. Without moving anything, Maris counted the heads — there were two or three cats, a dog, the goat, several chickens, a few sparrows, two crows and a barn owl. Some claws and hooves were also present.

She slammed the lid closed. "That's enough of that."

"What have we got?" Lauren asked.

"I suppose someone's sacrificial and ritual offerings. I really don't know," Wayne said.

"I know one thing," Maris said, "I'm damn glad that this is the DPS crime lab's rodeo and not mine. Someone needs to go through those things and photograph them, check the domestic animals for collars and take hair samples in case the information is needed later. I'd also have the lock fingerprinted. What a nasty job!" Standing, she batted away a fly and grinned at Lauren. "That'll be a good job for the rookie they hired for my old position."

"Maris, that's mean," Lauren said.

"I wish you were doing all of the crime scene work, Maris," Wayne said. "The DPS lab is backlogged and it's usually several weeks before I get a report from them. It's a good thing Lauren hired you to check the items she found in Karin's room and to go over the truck or we'd just now be getting them to the lab. It'd be weeks before we found out that it was goat blood on the blouse. But DPS won't let me use an outside service for something that our lab can do and both the Sheriff and the Chief said they can't pay."

"The lab is doing the best they can, Wayne. Unfortunately, they're still shorthanded and it takes a long time to get a new chemist trained. They're just overwhelmed with cases."

"I'm going to talk to the Ranger Captain about authorizing money for you to assist on crime scene investigations. Even if we send the evidence to DPS after you collect it, it'll help them save time since they won't have to stop working cases to cover the crime scene work. And I want the best, the most experienced."

"I appreciate that, Wayne. We need to be careful not to have evidence strung out with two or three different labs. Sometimes it's unavoidable in multi-jurisdiction cases, but we've almost missed some important details because of it."

"It couldn't be helped in this situation," Lauren said. "The police weren't taking Karin's disappearance seriously and missed the bloody blouse in their search of her room. They looked over Bobby Joe's truck before I came to Pierce and didn't notice the things Maris found. Since I have no official standing in this case, I was forced to use a private lab."

At Wayne's request, one of the deputies called the Blake house and left a message for the lab to come to the clearing when finished there. Ranger Coffey decided to take photographs and pick up some of the fresher cans and bottles for possible fingerprinting, as well as some of the newer cigarette butts. The DPS laboratory would check the fireplace for bloodstains.

Lauren and Maris drove in silence most of the way back to Pierce to pick up Lauren's car. Finally, Maris said, "I'm stumped. The evidence seems to indicate that Karin's body was transported in Bobby Joe's pickup, although I haven't typed the blood or looked at the fibers. If that works out as expected, what does all of this mean?"

"I don't know," Lauren said. "I feel like I'm no closer to finding out what happened to her than when I first came here. Now I'm debating on what I need to do next."

"I'm not too sure about the Satanism. We have innuendos and some evidence that it's real, but why are these stories just now coming out? Could this simply be a few kids dabbling in it for kicks?" Lauren nodded and Maris continued, "I think that our first suspect has to be Bobby Joe. He had more than one possible motive, the sexual abuse and the usual teenage conflicts. He killed her and disposed of the body."

"There's something else I found out, Maris. Bobby Joe may have had a lot to lose if Karin made any sexual abuse allegations against him. His trucking business is worth close to six million dollars, and he's recently entered an agreement with a partner to expand it even more by taking the company public. Any scandal at this stage could be devastating to him financially. I have to admit that, if he did it, he has certainly been cool about it."

"True," Maris said. "The boyfriend worries me. Maybe he really is into Satanism, or he's crazy and killed her. Jealousy may have played a role. He killed her and hid the body."

"Doesn't explain why Bobby Joe's Dodge was seen in town later. Where would he go, especially if he was drinking? And if it was Bobby Joe, why didn't Bennie arrest him for DWI?"

"Don't know, Lauren. What about this? Karin was having an affair with Bennie Wright, and he killed her. Maybe she was pregnant?"

"Sounds like we have lots of speculation, but not many facts. I still think Bobby Joe is involved."

"If Karin's dead, we need to find the body. If it's found soon, we'll have the answer to some of our questions. Until we find her, we have to assume that she could be still alive somewhere. Maybe she really did run away?"

Lauren sank lower in the corner of the pickup. She was pale and Maris could see the fear for Karin in her eyes. Maris wanted to stop the truck and hold her. Instead, she lightly touched her arm. Lauren

84

grabbed her hand and held it. "I'm running out of time. I think I'll start at the beginning with Karin's last known movements and retrace her steps by talking to all of the witnesses again. I've relied on Bennie Wright for some of the witness interviews, and I'm not sure that was a good idea."

"Then I'll go with you. One of those witnesses may be a murderer and Bennie may be pissed off since the Chief put him on desk duty. Where do you want to start?"

"Heather and Jennifer." Lauren took a notepad from her purse. Picking up Maris's mobile phone, she dialed. After a brief conversation, she said, "Jennifer is at Heather's. They'll talk to us if we drive out there. It's about three miles out of town."

Chapter Nine

Maris and Lauren easily found Heather's home. The brick house was about forty-two-hundred square feet with four or five bedrooms, Maris guessed. Wondering how people made that kind of money in Pierce, she drove into the driveway and stopped behind a new green Mustang convertible with the dealer tags.

Heather looked exactly like Maris expected when she answered the door bell — a blond, blue-eyed, bubble-gum-chewing teenager. Jennifer was her brown-eyed brunette twin.

After Lauren showed her badge and ID, the girls led them into a spacious den with a big-screen TV. The girls had been sitting on a beige L-shaped sectional sofa eating pizza and watching a movie. Maris had already decided she didn't have much patience for either of them, but the pizza made her hungry.

She sat next to Lauren on the sofa and asked, "Are your parents home?"

"Dad had a county commissioners' meeting tonight. Afterwards he and mother always go to the club for dinner."

"That your new car out front?" Maris snapped. Lauren frowned at her.

Jennifer giggled nervously. "It's mine. I got it for my sixteenth birthday."

"Does your dad know you're smoking dope in it and taking it to devil-worshiping ceremonies?" Maris asked, leaning closer to the girls.

"We aren't into the devil-worshiping," Heather said.

"No, we're not," Jennifer echoed.

"But you do drugs — pot, acid. How about XTC?"

"Look," Heather said. "I don't think we have to talk to you. My —"

Lauren pulled Maris back against the sofa. "We're not here about that. We're here about Karin's disappearance. But if you don't cooperate, we'll talk to your parents about the drugs. So, what do you know about Brian and his Satanic cult?"

The girls exchanged a glance. Heather nodded. "We'll tell you what we can. We don't run with that crowd much. We see Brian some because he's Karin's boyfriend, but we don't go out to the clearing."

Jennifer said, "We don't think any of the kids are serious about the devil worship. It's Brian that believes all of that stuff. The others just go along for the drugs and alcohol. We don't even believe the rumors about the orgies and sexual initiation rites. Karin wouldn't do any of that. She was angry when Brian tricked her into some weird ceremony with goat blood. But there was sex at the parties. We've heard the kids at school talk about it."

"No orgies, though," Jennifer said. "Just between boyfriend and girlfriend."

"What about the drugs?" Maris asked. "Did Karin take drugs?"

"Yes, whatever Brian had. But she wasn't an addict or anything." Heather made a face. "We don't really like Brian, but he and Karin have been close since grade school."

"She always stood up for him," Jennifer added. "Even when he became stranger and stranger."

"Were they intimate?" Lauren asked in a quiet voice.

Heather and Jennifer hesitated and Maris barked, "Did they have sex?"

"Oh, sure," Jennifer said. "But she had other boyfriends."

Heather shrugged. "She and Brian have had an on-again, off-again relationship for about two years."

"Who else did Karin date?" Lauren asked.

Heather looked down at her feet. Jennifer studied her hands. Maris said, "We think we know but we need you to confirm it."

"Bennie," Jennifer said quietly.

"For how long?" Lauren asked.

Tossing her dark hair, Jennifer said, "About a month, maybe."

"What did Brian think about this?" Maris asked. "Was he jealous?"

"I don't think so at first," Heather answered. "Karin said that he got off — thinking about her with other men. But Karin became so serious about Bennie. I think Brian was angry. We think it was more of Bennie's bullshit, but Karin swore they were going to get married. She left Devil's Leg with him the night she disappeared."

"Why haven't you told someone about this?" Lauren asked.

"No one would believe us over Bennie," Heather said.

"Yes," Jennifer added. "That's true, and we don't think Bennie had anything to do with her disappearance. He wouldn't hurt her."

"Why not?" Lauren asked. Because, Maris thought, he wasn't serious about her. Soon he'd have grown tired of her and moved on to another. She wondered if these girls had first hand experience.

Heather said, "He just wouldn't. He'd use her, but not hurt her."

Lauren sighed. "Where do you think Karin is?"

"We don't think she ran away from home," Heather answered, glancing at Jennifer. "We don't trust Brian."

"Could he have finally got jealous of Bennie and taken it out on Karin?" Maris asked, using a softer tone than she had before.

"We don't know, but we're afraid for her. And we miss her," Heather said.

They talked to the girls for several more minutes. Lauren made them give a detailed description of their activities for the Friday night Karin disappeared. She asked about Elaine Johnson. The girls knew who she was but didn't run with her.

When they left, Lauren called the police department and Bennie's home phone number but didn't find him. It was almost ten when Maris drove Lauren back to the S.O. to pick up her rented Taurus.

She asked, "Are you following me home?"

"I want to stop by Irene's, but I won't stay long."

"Are you sure you'll be okay?" Maris asked, holding her hand.

"I found those girls strangely depressing." She smiled. "I don't think you liked them at all."

"Well, it made a nice good-cop, bad-cop routine."

"They're just young — and spoiled. They're typical teenagers."

Maris watched her unlock the Taurus and get inside. When the brake lights came on, Maris started back to Allen. As the headlights swept across the city limit sign, she thought, What a fucked-up little town.

It was after midnight when Maris opened the back door and Earnhardt, barking with every step, ran inside. He returned with his tennis ball and threw it at Maris's feet as she pushed the button to play back the messages on the answering machine.

She smiled when she heard Kathy's voice. "Why aren't you in that lab working, Maris? I called to grill you about the good-looking redhead you were seen out with last night. Call and tell me your little secret, and I'll tell you how I heard about it. It's Tuesday, four o'clock. 'Bye."

"How the hell did she know?" Maris said, throwing the tennis ball down the hallway.

Several hang-up calls followed before a male voice said, "Lauren, honey, this is David. Why haven't you called and let me know what's happening down there? Your First National bank robbery case is going to court next Monday, and you're needed back by nine o'clock, Federal courthouse. Robert's prosecuting, and you know how persistent he is. I couldn't get him to postpone. I miss you. Let me know your travel arrangements. If I don't hear from you soon, I'm going to send the Dallas bureau after you. Call me."

Saving the message for Lauren, Maris felt the heat rise inside her as she turned away from the recorder. Was it her imagination or was there a certain familiarity in this guy's tone? Hadn't Lauren said that she had been single for a while? Maris had assumed she was separated from a woman. Uneasy and restless, she forced herself to work on the blood alcohol reports. Was she pushing it with Lauren? After all, her job and life were in Chicago, and sooner or later, she would return there, maybe sooner given the court case.

Maris, watching *Real Stories of the Highway Patrol*, heard Lauren's key turn in the front door lock. Earnhardt dashed to the door to meet her, and she stooped to greet him. Dropping her purse on the coffee table, she said, "Hello, I didn't think you'd be up?"

Trying to be impassive, Maris waited for Lauren

to come to her. Lauren's hair brushed her cheek when she leaned over Maris's chair to kiss her lips lightly. Maris resisted the urge to pull Lauren into her lap and forced herself to respond to the kiss coolly, despite her racing pulse.

"It took longer than I expected. What time is it?" Lauren said.

"About two-fifteen. You have an important message on the answering machine."

Maris winced when she heard Kathy's voice as Lauren played the messages. Damn it, she hadn't meant for Lauren to hear that. Lauren laughed. "I'll be paranoid now."

"Don't be paranoid about Kathy." She stopped talking as the man's voice started.

Maris turned to watch Lauren's reaction to the message. She faced away from Maris, but Maris saw her back stiffen. After the message ended, she asked, "How do you erase it?"

"Hit reverse," Maris said, resisting the urge to ask who the fuck David was. Give her a chance, an inner voice said, and Maris tried to push down the rising tide of anger that she felt inside. She knew she was overreacting, but pride wouldn't let her ask about this David.

"Damn, I thought that we'd get a plea on that case. Of all times for it to go to court." She came and sat down on the sofa. "I guess it's too late to call him tonight."

Maris sighed. She resolved not to do or say anything that she'd regret later, but she couldn't shake the feeling that Lauren knew more about her life than she knew about Lauren's. Maybe she was just tired. She stifled a yawn. "I'm going to take a quick shower and go to bed."

Lauren sighed. "I feel like time is running out and I still have more questions than answers. But it's too late to do anything else."

Maris woke up sweating, confused from a dream where she found Karin Beauchamp in a room full of goat heads and nude dancers in red devils' masks. She regained her bearings and found Lauren sitting on the side of the bed with her head buried in her hands. She may have been crying; Maris wasn't sure. She pulled herself upright and gently touched her shoulder.

"Lauren, honey, what's wrong?" she asked. Lauren turned and buried her head against Maris's neck. Hot tears splashed on her shoulder and rolled down to her chest, stinging her bare skin. She drew Lauren closer and felt the rise and fall of her breasts through the thin cotton nightshirt. The herbal odor of Lauren's shampoo aroused her as she nuzzled against Lauren's soft hair.

"What if we never know what happened?" Lauren asked. "What if we never know where she is, or if she's alive? With all of my training and your training and experience, why can't we find her?" Hesitating, she added, "Do you think she's dead?"

Maris sighed, wondering how she could best answer the question. "Honey, she's been missing for ten days now. You know the more time that passes without hearing from her the less likely it is we'll find her alive."

Maris slid over to give Lauren room to lie down. She ran her hand through Lauren's hair and down her cheek as she sobbed. Maris kissed her, tasting the salt from the tears.

After a while, Lauren returned her kisses with a sudden urgency that surprised Maris. They kissed passionately, and Maris stroked Lauren's breasts through the fabric of the T-shirt. She felt Lauren's nipple harden as she pinched it through the shirt. She wanted to feel Lauren's bare skin against hers and she nudged the T-shirt up until she could easily reach under it. Lauren grabbed Maris and pulled her close.

Lauren responded easily and quickly to her touch and opened up to accept Maris's hand. Lauren attempted to reach for Maris, but she gently pushed her away. She wanted nothing to interfere with the ecstasy she planned to give Lauren. The sheets were damp below Lauren's thighs when she finally went rigid and cried out. Maris held her until she heard Lauren's breathing return to normal.

Smiling, Lauren whispered, "Thank you," as her hand moved down to return the favor. Maris, already excited and aching for release, soon cried out.

They lay quietly with Lauren's head resting on Maris's chest for a long time. Maris realized that, at least for the moment, she was content. Breaking the silence, Lauren asked, "Maris, do you think it's possible to love more than one person . . . at the same time?"

Maris laughed and said, "Yes, I think so."

"So, you don't buy the theory that every person has that one true love put on earth for them alone?"

"Well, I loved Mary Ann and, in some ways, I think I'll always miss her. But, I don't think it means that I'll love any less intensely again. It's different though, each love is different. Besides, I'm not the person to ask — I fall in love two or three times a day."

"I'll bet Mary Ann had something to say about that." Lauren pinched Maris's side.

Squirming away, Maris said, "We had a 'look but don't touch' policy so it worked out."

"Then you do think it's possible to love two people at the same time?"

"Yeah, I think the heart can love more than one person at a time, but human emotions won't let the relationships exist in harmony for long. It's the dynamics of the triangle, the laws of chemistry and physics. There's too much energy stressing those bonds and sooner or later the weaker one will break. It's like a chemical compound with a three-membered ring — it takes very little outside stress to break the bonds apart, and when it happens..." Maris clapped her hands. Lauren jumped and Earnhardt pounced on the bed barking. "Boom, it can be explosive." Laughing, she said, "Get down, Earnhardt. It's okay."

Lauren giggled. "I should have known not to ask a chemist."

Rising up on one elbow, Maris asked, "Seriously, Lauren, why are you asking me this?"

"I was thinking about Karin and Brian. It wasn't a healthy relationship, but she always went back to him, and he always took her back. He knew about the other men."

"You can't judge by them. He's crazy and she's . . . troubled."

"Also, I'm wondering about us — where this is going. I'm afraid I could be jealous of Mary Ann."

Surprised, Maris said, "Why? I've tried to be careful not to talk about her too much. I don't compare you to her."

"Maybe not aloud, but you do. I feel like you've kept me at arm's length. You haven't once asked about my plans for the future, our plans for the future. What happens when I go back to Chicago? I'm not sure how you feel. You compliment me, but I don't know what you're really thinking. I thought we might be on the verge of something good here."

"We've only known each other three days. You know my situation, Lauren, but I don't know yours. We just don't know each other. Hell, I don't even know if you can cook, what your favorite color is, what your favorite movie is. I don't know these things yet. We're just getting to know each other."

"Maybe it's time for me to go back to Chicago for a while, to let each of us think about it. Maybe we're moving too fast."

Irritated, Maris asked, "Lauren, is there someone else?"

"No, I told you that I'd broken up with someone a few months ago. It's true. What if there was someone?" Lauren rolled over onto her side.

"I used to think I had all of the answers. Now, I don't know. I always told Mary Ann that I'd break us up in a New York minute if I caught her cheating. That is, if I didn't kill them both first. Especially, if she cheated with a man. To me, that seems much worse than another woman. It would

96

betray our lifestyle as well as me personally. But right after she died, I'd have taken her back no matter what the circumstances." Maris, tired of the conversation, pulled up the quilt and snuggled down into her pillow. "It seems that the answer to all of your questions is 'I don't know' and 'It depends.' How's that for a definite answer?"

"At least you have an answer," Lauren said as Maris cuddled behind her.

Chapter Ten

Lauren left for Chicago on Wednesday. Her sudden departure worried Maris, but Lauren claimed she needed the time in Chicago to handle her financial matters and to meet with the prosecutor for a pretrial conference. Maris spent the rest of the week lethargically catching up on her drug cases. Wednesday afternoon, the Garland Narcotics Task Force hit her with over thirty cases, including two hundred pounds of marijuana in twenty-five plastic-and-duct-tape-wrapped bundles, or bricks. She procrastinated on Lauren's evidence, using the drug cases as an excuse and, by Sunday morning, still had not examined the evidence from the Dodge.

It was another warm September Sunday, and Maris was unhappy, restless and lonely for Lauren — and Mary Ann — although thinking of one made her feel guilty about the other. Worse, Lauren had called only once since she left. Maris decided it was useless to try to work. She drove the red Oldsmobile convertible downtown to join the crowd gathered at the bar to watch the Cowboys play at three o'clock. Luckily, she found an open stool at the bar next to a former softball teammate and enjoyed her friendly conversation as the Cowboys won a close game over the Philadelphia Eagles.

On her way home, she stopped at a convenience store for a six pack of beer and a Sunday newspaper. She was home by eight o'clock and played the NASCAR race that recorded on her VCR while she was gone. Earnhardt ran through the house looking for Lauren before he settled down on the floor to chew on a rawhide bone. She had been home for a while before she noticed the light blinking on the answering machine.

The first message was from Lauren, and Maris, filled with an intense longing for her, initially regretted the missed telephone call. Stubbornly, she convinced herself it would do Lauren good to know she had places to go and things to do other than waiting at home for her to call. She decided not to call Lauren for one more night.

Several beeps on the recorder after Lauren's

message told Maris someone had called and hung up two or three times, and she let the tape keep running. After several more hang-ups, she reached out to rewind the tape but froze when a harsh, rasping voice ranted, "Fuck you, you bitch! The Evil One is not happy. You have desecrated sacred ground and you and the redhead are damned. You are damned! You are damned!"

There were two more calls, and several more hang-ups. The caller finally stopped his wild, profane ravings long enough to say he wanted the investigation in Pierce dropped. Maris pulled out the tape and replaced it with a new one. She debated about calling Wayne Coffey but decided not to bother him on a Sunday night. Instead, she inspected the .38 Smith and Wesson in the end table by her recliner and the Remington .12 gauge shotgun in the bedroom to make sure that each was clean and loaded.

The *Dallas Morning News* carried a long investigative report in the Sunday edition about the Satanic cult investigation in Pierce. She read the article and was agitated by the information. It was obviously intended to disturb the reader, and it did, although there was still no clear-cut evidence to back up the allegations. The teenager, who claimed to have delivered a baby for sacrifice, refused to name the father but insisted that he was a well-known figure in the community. Her true name was not given, but her stories correlated well with Elaine's.

New charges were made by children at a day care center where Brian Blake's aunt worked. Overwrought parents came forward after reports of the foster child, Cindy, and her story of sexual abuse were released in an earlier newspaper article. The parents claimed their children were despondent and having nightmares. An expert interviewed several of the children, and he claimed six children independently told him disturbing stories about Satanic rites and ritual sexual abuse. It reminded her of the McMartin Preschool hysteria. She still didn't know what to think about that case but was inclined to believe that where there's smoke there's fire.

Maris cut out the article and set it aside to send a copy to Lauren in Chicago. She hoped the media attention didn't interfere with the search for Karin Beauchamp. She couldn't get the article out of her mind. Clearly, there was some Satanic ritual abuse in Pierce county. She'd seen the autopsy photos of a young female murder victim found in a ditch in southern Johnson county. Her eyes were gouged out and there was mutilation of the genitalia. Satanic designs were carved into her breasts and stomach. Some officers and the local press were convinced she was the victim of a Satanic ritual. Her killer turned out to be a seventeen-year-old male classmate — acting alone. It did come out in the trial that he'd tampered with Satanic animal sacrifice, but there was no evidence of parental involvement or a cult. Could this be a similar case? she wondered.

She knew she needed to go to bed, but she dreaded sleeping alone. After Mary Ann's death, it took weeks for her to learn to sleep and live alone. It had taken only three days to get used to Lauren's presence, but now she was gone. Reluctantly, Maris prepared for bed. The telephone rang, and she grabbed it quickly, ready to blast the harassing caller and give the bastard a cussing lesson. She was surprised to hear, instead, the slow drawl of Deputy Ralph Lambert.

"Maris," he said. "Bennie Wright's dead. It looks like a gun-cleaning accident, but we're not sure. Wayne said to call you and have you come down to look at the blood-spatter evidence. He's in Austin at the DPS Academy and won't be back until late Tuesday."

Suddenly wide awake, Maris asked, "When did this happen?"

"A neighbor found him about an hour ago. The body's still here."

"Try not to move anything, and I'll be there as soon as I can." She scribbled directions to the house and was almost ready to hang up when she remembered the calls. "Ralph, I've been getting some threatening calls tonight about the investigation. I'll bring the tape with me."

There was a pause, and he said, "Be careful, Maris. There were some strange calls on Bennie's answering machine, and now he's dead. Watch yourself."

Maris easily found Bennie Wright's mobile home in Pierce. It was only a few blocks from the store where Karin met her stepdad the night she disappeared. Three sheriff's department cars and two Pierce police cars were parked in front. The first P.D. car in the driveway was probably Bennie's. The other had to be Chief Wilkes's.

Maris parked as close as she could and checked

the film in her camera. She glanced at her watch and noted that it was a quarter after midnight. She jotted the time down in her notebook, picked up her investigation kit and walked toward the door of the trailer. Two deputies talked quietly near the steps with Chief Wilkes.

"Hello, Chief," Maris said, "I'm sorry to hear about Bennie. I know you were close."

"Thanks, Maris, I can't believe it was a gun accident. He was too careful for a mistake like that." He opened the door and held it for Maris.

She smelled the blood when she entered the small living room. Bennie was in the kitchen on the floor next to an overturned chair. As she approached carefully, Maris saw a gun-cleaning kit and a Colt .45 semi-automatic pistol on the table. Deputy Ralph Lambert stood at the kitchen counter taking notes, talking to another deputy. The other deputy left when he saw Maris.

"Maris," he said, "thanks for coming. You didn't have anything planned anyway, did you?"

"Just sleeping, Ralph. Is this the way you found him?" She set her kit on the floor outside of the kitchen, opened it and put on a pair of latex gloves. She also slipped a pair of plastic covers over the bottom of her shoes. She was dismayed to see that Ralph and the other deputy were not wearing shoe covers.

"Yes, nothing's been moved here. We've fingerprinted some items in the other room, but nothing in here yet. A neighbor came over to see him and found the door open. As soon as he stepped inside, he saw him and went back out and called us."

Maris nodded. Even to the untrained, it was

obvious that Bennie Wright didn't need any medical attention. Half of the back of his head was missing. "Any idea what time he died?" she asked.

Ralph pointed to the area behind the fallen chair. Maris walked carefully around the body to the opposite end of the table. "Can you believe it?" Ralph said. "Just like the movies." He pointed to a small battery-operated kitchen clock, shaped like a cutting board with two black hands. It rested face up on the white kitchen tile about three feet from the over-turned chair. It appeared to have fallen from a hook on the wall directly behind the chair. Blood spatters, bone fragments and brain matter covered the wall around where the clock used to be, as well as the face of the clock on the floor, leaving a clear white circle on the wall with an empty hook in the center. A large piece of skull littered the floor not far from the clock. A bullet fragment was embedded in the wood near the number six. The time read four thirty-five.

"In all of my years in law enforcement, I've never had a stopped clock or wristwatch to help me determine the time of death." Ralph shook his head in amazement.

"I haven't either, Ralph." Looking around the kitchen, Maris asked, "What about shoeprints? How many people have traipsed through here?"

He looked down at his boots guiltily. "Too many of us."

"It may not be too late. Kitchen tile is a good background for finding prints. I might still find some partials that could be useful if this turns out not to be an accident. I'll need to get known impressions from everyone who's been in here." Maris tried to keep her irritation from sounding in her voice. Why did even the more thorough investigators routinely overlook the possibility of shoeprints at a scene? she wondered. "Let me get started on the blood spatters. We'll see what story they tell us. If it appears to be an accident, we won't need to look for shoeprints."

"It doesn't sound like Bennie to be careless. If you'll do the crime scene analysis, we'll send the gun and any other evidence to the DPS lab."

Maris started by writing a detailed description of the room and the location of the body and other items. A deputy brought her tripod from the pickup while she finished her notes, and she shot two rolls of film doing an overview of the crime scene and the body. With the tripod, she shot more detailed photographs, complete with a scale, of the blood spatters behind the fallen chair.

Once she completed the photographs, she measured several stains on the back wall and wrote the figures in her notebook. Using mathematical formulas that she carried with her on a laminated card, she determined the location of the source of the blood spatters at the time of bullet impact, revealing the position of Bennie Wright's head when the shot was fired.

"How tall was he?" she asked, standing near the spot her calculations indicated as the probable point of origin of the blood spatters.

"About six feet or so." Ralph shrugged.

Using a tape measure, Maris measured from a point on the floor up to an invisible point in the air near her nose. She wrote the figures in her notebook. Several officers crowded the kitchen doorway and watched intently. She stepped over the body and knelt down on the floor next to the dead officer. The bullet, it appeared, entered near his left nostril, above his upper lip. She thought she saw some tattooing around the entrance wound, indicating that the barrel was very close to his face when it was fired, but she couldn't see very well in the kitchen light and Bennie wore a mustache.

"Okay, boys," she said, "I'm going to have to start moving things around a little. Anything you want to do before I disturb the body?"

"Go ahead," Ralph said. "Let us know if you need any help."

Maris nodded. Without moving the body, she examined his fingers, back of his hand and his wrist using a small magnifying glass from her pocket. Before she rolled him over, she noticed some small rivulets of blood that streamed from the bullet hole. They'd need the autopsy report to be sure, but she suspected that the angle of entry was slightly upwards. She snapped a close-up of the wound and jotted down more notes before she rolled the body over, with Ralph's help, and looked at Bennie's left hand. When satisfied, she placed small brown paper sacks from her investigation kit over each hand and secured them with thick rubber bands.

"He's all yours," she said, and Ralph motioned to one of the deputies. "Be sure that you have his hands examined for gunshot residue."

Moving to the other side of the body, she leaned over to look at the .45 Colt. The clip had been removed and a cleaning rag and gun barrel cleaning swab rested next to the gun. She noticed tiny blood droplets on the top portion of the gun. She took close-up photographs of the pistol and paused, moving to one side, while two attendants loaded the body into a body bag and carried him outside to a hearse for transportation to the medical examiner.

When they were out of the way, she used cotton swabs to remove some of the tiny blood stains from inside the gun barrel.

"You can have the gun," she said, "I haven't touched it except where I removed the blood stains. Maybe you can get some prints." Moving toward the kitchen sink, she asked, "Has anyone used this sink since you've been here?"

"Not as far as I know," Ralph said.

She had Ralph turn out the lights and she sprayed the basin and drain with the Luminol reagent. She immediately saw a small area around the drain that glowed weakly.

"Wow," Ralph said, looking over her shoulder, "how about that?"

"Turn on the lights, please," Maris said. "You were right, Ralph. Bennie probably didn't have an accident or commit suicide. When the bullet went through him, it dispersed a cone of high-velocity blood droplets out the exit wound. Anything close enough to the entry wound will be covered in a fine mist of blood from the spatter effect."

She paused and looked at the overturned chair. "In my opinion, Bennie's head, or the point of origin for the bloodstains on the wall, was here." She held her hand up even with her nose. "Too high for him to be sitting in a chair. He was standing and someone put the gun up close to his face, like this." She demonstrated with her right hand cocked like a gun. "The assailant shot him at almost point-blank range. The backspatter covered the top of the gun and even splashed into the barrel. It probably covered the hand of the person holding the gun as well. It may even be on his cuff if he was wearing a long-sleeved shirt. I didn't see any blood on Bennie's hands. Also, look at the floor here." She gestured to where the body had been located. "See these faint smears — there may be a partial shoeprint here. I think the body was moved forward and turned slightly in an attempt to make it look like he was sitting in the chair cleaning his gun. In reality, he was probably standing about here."

"Then the murderer put the gun on the table and went to the sink to wash the blood off of his hands," Ralph added.

"Yeah."

Abruptly, a young deputy pushed his way through the group of men standing in the kitchen doorway. "Ralph," he said, "I just talked to the old lady across the street. Man, she's really upset about Bennie's death, but she finally calmed down enough to talk to me and the Chief. She says that Bobby Joe Beauchamp came to visit Bennie this afternoon. She remembers it clearly because she was surprised to see Bobby Joe. She usually sees Irene Beauchamp instead. She figured it was something to do with the search for Karin. She said that Bennie told her that they were having lots of trouble with Karin before she disappeared, and Irene often came over to talk to him about her. She says that the youth and parents of this town will miss Bennie Wright."

"No doubt," Maris said.

"Yeah, especially the girls," another deputy added.

Maris sprayed the floor tile with amido black where she thought someone might have walked to move the chair and Bennie's body. At least seven overlapping bloody shoeprint impressions, invisible to the naked eye, were well-defined when enhanced. Maris saw one wavy sole pattern design consistent with a work boot. The others looked like they were left by the smooth leather soles of the cowboy boots Ralph and his deputies wore.

She pointed. "You need to find out if Bobby Joe wears this kind of work boot."

Other shoeprints, some of them with the wavy design, made a trail to the sink. She sprayed the doorway and more faint bloody shoeprints appeared, mostly from the wavy sole pattern designed with a few boot prints. The shoeprints grew fainter and finally disappeared halfway down the hall.

Maris documented the position and direction of the prints and took comparison-quality photographs. When finished, she said, "Ralph, the shooting may not have been premeditated. I think there was an argument and somehow the killer got hold of Bennie's gun. These prints were made as the killer went down the hallway to find the gun-cleaning kit to make it look like Bennie shot himself by accident. If you can get me the boots, I may be able to tie them to some of these prints by the wear marks and cuts on the sole."

Maris packed up her supplies and left the scene shortly after two-thirty, Monday morning. It was cool outside, and she used the heater in her truck for the first time this fall. She stopped at the little store and bought a cup of coffee, a pint of chocolate milk and a Hostess fried apple pie to help keep her awake as she drove home. So Bobby Joe Beauchamp may have killed Bennie Wright, she thought. They would be questioning him soon. She had to get to work on the evidence from Bobby Joe's Dodge pickup. If they put pressure on him about Bennie Wright's murder, he might confess to Karin's as well. Maybe the bastard would tell them where he hid the body.

She ought to have her ass kicked for procrastinating on the Beauchamp evidence. Why had she done that? It wasn't like her. Oh, hell, who was she kidding? She had postponed the analysis because the case made her painfully aware how much she missed Lauren, and she couldn't stand it.

Chapter Eleven

After only four hours sleep, Maris stumbled into the laboratory. Monday morning would be dedicated to the Karin Beauchamp evidence from Bobby Joe's pickup. She started with the photographs. The most intriguing ones were of the stain in the pickup bed as it luminesced from the Luminol.

She picked up a magnifying glass and studied the photograph under bright light. The pattern of the fabric weave showed a line down one side with two circles in the corner. Lauren was right. It was the corner of a tarp.

Maris drove to a camera shop nearby with the self-service equipment necessary for her to blow up the photograph, or portion of the photograph, from the negative. It was expensive, requiring trial and error to obtain a shot true in size to scale, but in a couple of hours she had expanded the photographs of the stains in the back of the pickup and the thumbprint on the steering wheel.

Around noon she decided to call Chicago and leave a message for Lauren. She called the number Lauren left for her and listened with irritation as the male voice droned out the usual message.

"Who the fuck are you?" she said after she left the message and slammed down the phone. She called the Chicago FBI office, and the secretary agreed to page Lauren for her. Maris was surprised to catch someone at lunch time and even more surprised when Lauren called within fifteen minutes.

"You call, lover?" Lauren said, laughing.

Maris felt a rush of excitement, but she forced herself to speak calmly. "I wanted to tell you that Bennie Wright was killed last night."

"You're kidding! Really?"

"Yes, they tried to make it look like an accident, but it was murder. I did the investigation. Didn't get home until late last night, actually early this morning."

"Do they have a suspect yet?"

"Bobby Joe. A neighbor lady saw him at Bennie's home. She puts him there at the time of death."

"My God, I wonder why he'd do it."

"I don't know. I also wanted to tell you about an article in yesterday's paper, a story about the investigation in Pierce and the allegations about the Satanic cults. Seems hysteria is taking over the town. It'll be worse now that Bennie's dead. When will you be back?"

"Soon as possible. The trial is almost over. Should be finished by Wednesday. My bureau chief is getting impatient, but with the family leave plan, he has to let me have a full six weeks. I hope I'm not wasting it. I don't have the money to stay off work much longer. With luck, if they arrest Bobby Joe on Bennie's murder, we'll find out what happened to Karin." Lauren sighed. After a pause, she added, "I've missed you, Maris Middleton."

After talking to Lauren, Maris found it hard to concentrate as she mounted the blue fibers from the fifth-wheel trailer hitch on microscope slides. She identified nylon. Next, she turned to the samples that were lifted with the clear tape from the front of the pickup. She observed numerous orange, white and black fibers on the tape. She mounted some of the fibers on a microscope slide and peered through the lens. The orange, white and black fibers were a mixture of polyester and cotton, consistent with a T-shirt.

She studied her notes. Lauren's sister thought Karin was wearing a T-shirt with the high school mascot, a tiger, on the front. The school's colors were orange and black. But how, Maris wondered, did the fibers get on the front of the pickup? Did she lean against the front fender? Maybe, but that wouldn't explain the dent. Was she slammed against the fender during a violent argument? Or, although it seemed unlikely, was she run over by the truck?

Next, came the fibers from the woodpile. They were microscopically similar to the blue fibers found on the trailer hitch in the pickup bed. Did someone remove the tarp from the woodpile and use it to transport Karin's body in the back of the truck?

When she finished with the fibers, Maris turned her attention to the dark brown stain from the back of the pickup. She set up the tests to determine if it was human blood and froze a sample for later DNA testing. Before she could start a drug case, the telephone rang. She grabbed it and recognized Ranger Wayne Coffey's slow drawl.

"Hello, Wayne, I was thinking about calling you in Austin. You're not telepathic are you?"

"Shit, no, if I was I'd know what the hell was going on in this damned county. Maris, I flew back early this morning, and I'm in Pierce now. I called because we found the body, we think, in the bottom of an old abandoned well only six miles from Brian Blake's house."

"Poor thing, I'm glad we finally found her. Is the body wrapped in a blue tarp?"

There was a long pause before Wayne answered, "How did you know that?"

"So it is in a blue tarp."

"Looks like it from what we can see looking down in the well. It must be important to something you've found."

Quickly, Maris explained the results of her examinations on the evidence from Bobby Joe's Dodge pickup. "Also," she added, "I've found white, orange and black polyester and cotton fibers on the front fender of the truck near a dent and probable bloodstain. I'm going to need the clothes and the tarp if it's Karin in the bottom of the well. Do you mind if I come out to the scene, Wayne?"

114

"No, I was going to ask you to come out and help us, but I figured you're worn out after last night. Ralph told me about Bennie. Thanks for the help. We've got a shitty job ahead. I asked the DPS lab to come out, but the supervisor said none of his people was going down into the bottom of that well."

"Sounds about right."

"This county has a contract with a pathologist in Tyler to do all of their autopsies, but of course he has no field team. He won't come out."

"I'll be there as soon as I can. It'll take me a little over two hours to load my equipment and drive out there. I don't have a self-contained breathing device, but I have some protective respirators."

"I think there's plenty of air down there, but bring anything that'll help with the dust and odor. Don't forget the mentholatum. Where's the lady FBI agent?"

"Federal court, in Chicago."

"Just as well. She doesn't need to see her niece like this." He told her how to find the location, and she quickly checked and resupplied her kit, loaded her camera and shut down the lab. She packed a box with protective clothing and stacked the equipment in her pickup.

A county squad car waited for her on the paved road near the cattle guard, and the officer instructed her to follow a rough dirt road down to the well. Several men, leaning against their cars, waited patiently in the dusty pasture about thirty yards from the well. Maris's pickup kicked up clouds of dust as she pulled to a stop near the other vehicles. A small red pumper truck from the local fire department was parked much closer to the well, but the firemen waited with the other men. As she climbed out of her truck, Ranger Coffey approached, dressed in his yellow Nomex coveralls and wearing latex gloves. The suits, designed to be impervious to most chemicals and body fluids, were stifling hot. Looking like a large ruffled canary, he stopped and wiped his flushed face with his sleeve.

"Hello, gentlemen," Maris called out to the others as she met the Ranger part way. With each breath, she smelled the sickly sweet odor of the putrid body. It would be much worse in the bottom of the well. "Wayne, after I get ready, I want to take a quick look from the top and snap some pictures. How big is the bottom of the well?"

"I figure that it's about six feet in diameter, but you don't have to go down there with me, Maris. It's damp, nasty and cramped," Wayne said frowning. He obviously didn't relish the idea.

Maris looked around. The firemen would probably go, but they were volunteers, and judging from the beer bellies, not in the best of shape. Chief Deputy Ralph Lambert was not present, and the two green-faced young deputies looked like they already had all they could handle. "No, I'll go, Wayne. That's why I'm here, and it looks like I'm the best prepared."

She opened the camper and tailgate and checked the camera. She pulled a pair of yellow Nomex coveralls on over her jeans and T-shirt and slipped thick plastic foot covers over her shoes. She taped the foot covers to the bottom of her coveralls and helped

Wayne tape his. She picked up a charcoal-filtered respirator to help protect her from the dust and stench when she descended into the well. She took two pairs of latex gloves and double-gloved her hands.

Waiting patiently, Wayne said, "The fire boys'll help us rappel down the side of the well, using a winch to lower us and bring us up. We'll each wear a line the whole time we're down there, in case we get into trouble and they have to get us out fast. We'll put the body in a body bag and attach a line for them to pull it to the top."

"Hope you have an extra body bag with you. If I get down there and find a bunch of snakes, I'll have a damned heart attack."

"Don't say that, Maris. I hate those fucking snakes as bad as you do."

As they approached in their bright yellow protective suits, one of the fireman called out, "Ya'll sure make a cute couple." Everyone laughed nervously. The well, made of natural stone, appeared to be very old. A piece of tin and some boards, once covering the well, lay on the ground to the side.

As Maris took some pictures, she asked, "How'd you find it?"

"Usual way. Hunters. They were setting up their stands and feeders. After smelling the odor, they noticed that the tin cover on the well had been removed and decided to look inside. Somebody had a flashlight and they could see the body wrapped in a blue tarp. One of them called the S.O. from the service station at the intersection, a mile west."

Once Maris completed her sketch, made some notes and photographed the well, she stood on tiptoe and leaned over the side, peering down the shaft.

The fire department had suspended strong spotlights, powered by a diesel generator, inside the well. The mentholatum in her nose and the respirator could not block all of the putrid odor that assailed her as she leaned over the edge. The tarp was secured around the body with bungee cords and gray duct tape. She made a mental note to tell the pathologist to take care of the tape. She might be able to match a torn end of it with the roll it came from, if the rest of the roll was still in the killer's possession. The body, in a sitting position, leaned awkwardly with the head propped against the wall of the well. To Maris's relief, the only standing water covered the half of the well floor across from the body. She hoped that it didn't disguise a drop off and that the floor was solid. She snapped some pictures and made a quick sketch of the body's position and location.

"Let's do it." She raised her arms for one of the firemen to attach the safety line around her waist. They'd already placed one around Wayne. She secured the camera around her neck and hoisted herself up on the side of the well.

"Let me go first, Maris," Wayne said.

"No, I think I should. I'm a little smaller and lighter. I'll holler at you or signal when I'm ready for you to come down. This way I'll have more room to take pictures."

"Anything seems not right, you jerk on the line, and we'll get you out of there."

She nodded and pulled the respirator into place. I can do this, she told herself, turning on her stomach as she lowered her feet. She had never rappelled before, but managed a fair imitation. Luckily, the firemen fed the line slowly. She dropped about fifteen feet. Her heart was pounding when her foot touched the bottom, but it felt solid, if slippery. The firemen fed her a couple of feet of spare line, and after removing the respirator, she took some photographs. If these lights go out, she thought, I'll climb this fucking line so fast it'll catch fire.

She saw and heard crickets, scorpions and other insects scurrying around the bottom of the well. As she focused the camera, she struggled to maintain her balance on the well bottom, slimy with water and body grease. The blue tarp was wet and stained. Stray strands of blond hair spilled out of several holes. A bloated finger, with a dirty rose-colored fingernail, pointed accusingly out of a tear near the middle of the body. When she completed the shots, she signaled to Wayne, and he started his descent. She put her respirator back into place. Waiting for Wayne to arrive was terrible as she fought a bout of claustrophobia.

When Wayne hit bottom, the firemen dropped a black plastic body bag down. Maris unzipped it, and they positioned the bag on the floor near the body. Sweating profusely, she struggled to see through the fogged lens of the respirator. They worked the bag under the body and clumsily changed places in the cramped space so the Ranger could lift the heavy upper body and Maris the feet. As gently as possible, they lifted the body high enough to slide it in. Although not Catholic or even particularly religious, she felt a strong urge to make the sign of the cross as she zipped the black body bag.

Getting the body to the surface was more difficult. They finally strapped it to a backboard, and the firemen pulled it up. It spun awkwardly, banging against the side of the well until it reached the top. Maris waited until it was safely on the surface before taking more pictures. She and Wayne scoured the floor of the well but found nothing of interest. He insisted the firemen pull Maris up first.

As she untied the safety line, she watched a firemen and a mortician load the body into a hearse for the trip to the pathologist's office in Tyler. The mood of the group was somber as Wayne and Maris walked to her truck and removed their protective clothing. Maris placed both sets of clothing into a black trash bag. It was now biohazardous material and required special disposition. Using sterile wipes, they cleaned their hands and faces. Neither spoke until they were finished, and one of the deputies handed them each a cold bottle of Gatorade. Maris accepted it gratefully.

"I talked to the pathologist after I called you, Maris. He's agreed to do the autopsy today and identify the body as soon as possible, so we can notify the family. I made him feel guilty, I think. Do you want to come with me to witness it?"

No, not really, she thought, but she replied, "Yes, I'll follow you if you promise to drive like a normal person and not a Ranger." A Ranger didn't call it fast until he passed a hundred on the speedometer. Maris prudently tried to stay under ninety.

He smiled. "I promise not to lose you."

"Ordinarily, I wouldn't have to go with you, but I need to tell him what I found on the pickup. It's possible she was hit by the Dodge. While I'm there, he can release the tarp, duct tape, clothing and a blood and tissue sample to me right away."

Dreading the autopsy, she turned the truck and

tucked in behind the Ranger's maroon Chevrolet Caprice. She thought of Lauren and knew that she'd miss her very much when she arrived home from Tyler.

Chapter Twelve

Tired, Maris stretched the tarp out on the examining table and placed Karin's clothing, including her shoes, under the ventilation hood for them to dry overnight. After locking the lab, and hoping the ventilation hood kept the odor out of the house, Maris stripped in front of the washer and placed every stitch of clothing inside with a strong dose of bleach. She scrubbed her hands well enough to grab a beer out of the refrigerator. Popping the top on the way to the shower, she drank half of it as she started the water and adjusted the temperature as hot as she could stand it. She finished the rest of the cold Miller Lite as the hot water pounded her back.

Fortified, Maris washed her hair and body three times and stood there until she began to run out of hot water. The unpleasant sight of the putrefying body and the gore of the autopsy were tolerable, but there was no escaping the odor. She wondered if she'd ever get the smell out of her pickup. At least, the body was not burned, and it was more intact than Maris expected. Most of the damage was from insects, mice and rats, since the well protected the body from the larger carnivores. Yet the blond hair was all that remained to hint of the beautiful teenage girl who had once lived.

Perhaps, the most disturbing aspect of the entire day was the preliminary results of the autopsy. Maris had guessed right. Karin may have been run over by the pickup, but it didn't kill her. The pathologist was sure that she was alive when she was dumped into the well — badly injured, bleeding internally, but still alive. She and Wayne couldn't see how Karin managed to draw a ragged breath through the tightly wrapped tarp, but the pathologist insisted she had. There were secondary injuries from the fall into the well. Maris hoped that Karin Beauchamp, when placed into the tarp, was already unconscious and remained so when she was dumped like so much trash. Mercifully, the pathologist thought, but couldn't promise, that the injuries from the fall ended her suffering quickly. She could have lingered, could have been in and out of consciousness, and could have died a slow, lonely death.

It was almost one o'clock in the morning when Maris went to the back door to let Earnhardt inside.

He didn't understand the delay but was overjoyed to see her. She checked her answering machine and saw the message light flashing. She pushed the button and heard the tape back up while she went into the kitchen to get a second beer. Mary Ann, when she was alive, always fixed Maris a grilled cheese sandwich after a late-night investigation and had it waiting for her when she finished her shower. She suddenly felt lonely. She stood by the answering machine and heard the same guttural voice shout obscenities and talk wildly about desecration and burning in hell. Too tired to care, she pushed the fast forward button until she was past the first message. When she stopped the tape, she heard a tearful message from Lauren asking her to call regardless of the time. Hoping she really meant it, Maris dialed the number.

The phone rang once before it was answered. "Lauren? How are you doing?"

"Managing. I thought I'd prepared myself for the worst, but when it finally came, I wasn't as prepared as I thought. It was her, wasn't it."

"Well, honey, they called her dentist in Tyler, and a trooper ran her dental records over for the pathologist. I'm sure it's her. I'm sorry."

"Thank you. The prosecutor said that I could leave tomorrow afternoon to return to Dallas. I haven't booked a flight yet."

"Let me pick you up, Lauren. We can get you a rental car later."

"No, I'll need it early the next morning to go to Pierce. I still have your house key." Too tired to talk any longer, they said their good-byes and hung up. Maris finished her beer and went to bed.

* * * * *

Rising early Tuesday morning, Maris ate a quick bowl of cereal and drank two cups of coffee. She didn't even bother to shower again, knowing she would spend the day working with the clothes and tarp from Karin's body. It didn't promise to be pleasant. The clothing was slimy with body fluids and grease. Drying them didn't help the odor, but it helped stop the rapid deterioration of the blood and other evidence.

Examining the tarp, she found the corner that matched the stain in the back of the pickup. She documented her work and took more photographs. It was her opinion that the tarp had been in the back of Bobby Joe's pickup. There was a large area of brown dried blood on one side of the tarp. The blood must have leaked through the tarp and gathered on the bed of the truck. Then, as the truck was driven, the backdraft must have flipped the corner of the tarp over into the blood that was probably drying quickly. There were small pieces of bark and wood fiber present over most of the inside of the tarp. She expected to find oak and pecan fibers consistent with the kind in the Beauchamps' firewood stack.

Maris examined the clothing for paint from the Dodge, but found none. Karin's personal items were still in the pockets of her jeans, and Maris set these things aside to inventory and package for release to Wayne and eventually to the family. Inside a front pocket, Maris found a small piece of folded foil paper. She recognized the contents immediately as two hits of Beavis and Butthead LSD papers. When she had time, she'd test them for the presence of LSD. She hoped any LSD present was protected by the foil paper from the dampness of the rotting body.

The telephone interrupted her thoughts, and she resentfully answered it. It was Leona, the DPS laboratory secretary, and she started by apologizing. "Maris, sorry to call like this, but I promised that I'd try to find you. Denton county called, and they need you for court." She paused and added, "Today."

"Today!" Maris glanced at the clock. It was already ten-fifteen. It would be noon before she could shower, dress and drive to Denton.

Leona hesitated. "Actually, they notified us earlier, but the message was misplaced. It was never placed on the calendar, and we failed to call you."

"Okay, I'll go, but it'll take me about an hour to get ready and come out there to get the records." She quickly secured the evidence and went to shower and dress.

Maris thought she made a good impression on the jury with her red blouse, black trousers, gray Western-style blazer and black eel Tony Llama boots. The testimony was routine: yes, it was cocaine; yes, it was in the crack form; yes, it was less than a gram in weight; no questions from the defense. Still, it was five-fifteen before she left the stand. Traffic was unusually snarled, and it was a quarter to seven before she arrived home. Her heart leapt when she saw a black Chevrolet Lumina in the driveway. It had to be Lauren's rental car.

In a rush, she unlocked the front door. Startled to hear a male voice and seeing no one in the living room, she started down the hallway. Turning the corner, she felt and smelled the steam from a recent shower as it escaped from the partially open door of the front bathroom. Lauren stood in the guest bedroom hugging a man wearing jeans, but no shirt or socks. He was of medium height, handsome, not particularly muscular but fit, with dark brown, neatly trimmed hair. As he stood with a towel around his neck and the remnants of shaving cream on his cheek, Lauren casually pet the curly brown hair on his bare chest as she hugged him. He laughed as if he had made a joke, and Lauren said to him, "I'm glad you decided to make this trip with me, despite the hard feelings in the family."

The anger in Maris was instantaneous.

Lauren caught her movement in the hallway and smiled. "Hello, Maris, where've you been?" She stepped forward, but stopped short when Maris exploded.

"Who the fuck is this, and what the hell do you mean bringing him here? Especially after our discussion. God damn, I can't believe it!" Maris felt the uncontrollable urge to hit something as she whirled and stalked back down the hall. The bathroom door caught her eye, and she lashed out with a savage kick. She knocked the door back against the wall with such force that it sprang forward, and she belted it with a right hook. This happened two more times before she gave up trying to kill the door and stomped into the living room.

She heard a stunned Lauren say, "Maris, what's wrong with you? You're scaring me!"

"God damn, you better get him out of my house, or you'll both have something to be scared about."

"It's not what you think!"

"Shit, you have some nerve."

"He's my brother!"

Maris turned and saw the man laughing as he stood in the hallway near the living room. He said, "This one has spirit, Lauren. They say people with terrible tempers make passionate lovers. She's much more interesting than your last. I think you should definitely keep her."

Lauren burst into tears, brushing past him as he threw his hands up and mockingly squeezed against the wall for her to pass. She slammed the door to Maris's bedroom, knocking a photograph of Maris's grandmother off the hallway wall.

"Jesus Christ!" Maris exclaimed. She'd really done it now. Her fucking brother? Looking at him, she knew it was true. The resemblance, especially in his eyes and mouth as he laughed, was unmistakable. "Why didn't she tell me she had a fucking brother?"

"I'm David O'Conner," he said, ignoring the remark. He laughed again as he extended his hand.

"Her brother, huh?" Maris said, rapidly deflating.

"Yes, I'm afraid so."

"Oh Lord," she groaned, "forgive me for making such an ass of myself. Excuse me . . . while I go plead temporary insanity."

He nodded as she stepped past him to the bedroom. The sound of weeping made her chest ache. She closed the door softly behind her. Lauren, on her side of the bed, sat bent with her face buried in a pillow pressed to her face. Maris knelt down in front of her, fighting tears herself. She gently wrapped her hands around Lauren's wrists and pulled the pillow away from her face. Lauren's eyes, puffy and red from the lack of sleep and tears for Karin, glistened and spilled fresh tears.

"I'm sorry," Maris said softly.

"Maris, your timing is great. I don't need this little display of possession right now." She sniffed, shook Maris's hands off and angrily reached for a tissue on the bedside table.

"I overreacted. Something's seemed funny, strained between us. Damn it, Lauren, it's just that you know my situation, but... there seemed to be more than court pulling you back to Chicago."

"I told you I wasn't with anyone."

"I know you did. You said it was a recent breakup, three months, I think. I don't know why I acted like that. I've had the feeling that you're holding back, like there's something you haven't told me." Maris caught her hands again and held them. "I'm sorry."

"You scared me. I don't know if I can take that kind of jealousy."

There was a soft knock on the door, and David cracked it a couple of inches. "It sure is quiet in here. Did you make up fast, or kill each other?"

"We're talking," Lauren sniffled. "I'll be out in a minute to finish getting ready." To Maris, she said, lowering her voice, "We were waiting for you to come home and go to dinner with us. I wanted you to meet David before we drove to Pierce."

Her knees aching, Maris rose and sat on the bed next to Lauren. Putting her arms around her, Maris pulled her close and said, "Please forgive me. I missed you so much, Lauren. So did Earnhardt." Maris cupped her chin and kissed her tenderly.

Lauren didn't resist, but neither was she

responsive. Standing, Lauren sighed. "I have to get ready."

Maris's heart dropped as Lauren stood and walked out of the bedroom. She heard David say, "Lauren, don't make a mistake." She couldn't hear Lauren, but David said, "Why didn't you tell her about me?" Lauren replied something about trust in a relationship, and David's deeper male voice echoed in the hallway. "She senses you haven't told her everything. I think this is partly your fault!"

If Lauren responded, Maris didn't hear her. She changed clothes, putting on a T-shirt and sweats. Flopping on her back with her hands clasped tightly behind her head, she lay on the bed and listened, following Lauren's and David's movements as they prepared to leave. As the front door closed and the dead bolt clicked into place, she wondered if they would return to spend the night or stay in Pierce.

Chapter Thirteen

After a miserable evening spent moping, Maris went to bed early to lie awake and dissect her life. It was late when she heard murmured voices and saw lights go on and off in the living room, bathroom and guest room. She waited, not daring to hope, wondering where Lauren would sleep. Relief flooded over her when she heard someone enter the room and felt the bed give as Lauren slid underneath the sheet. Maris rolled over and touched her shoulder. Lauren kept her back to Maris, and Maris ran her hand soothingly down Lauren's side. She was surprised to feel the panties that Lauren wore under her nightshirt.

"Lauren, I'm sorry about this evening."

"I know, Maris." Lauren rolled over onto her back and light from the window reflected off her red hair.

Maris caressed her hair. "I love you, Lauren. I don't want to lose you," Maris said, her voice cracking.

"Oh, Maris," Lauren sighed. "Your timing sucks."

"I know, but —"

"Before you say anything else," Lauren said, placing her fingertips on Maris's lips. "You're right when you say you sense something else. No, don't say anything, listen. I met my first lover in college. We broke up before I went to law school. After that I was too busy for anything serious, and I was already thinking about the FBI. I worried about the background check until I met a young attorney, Robert, who was handsome and less oppressive — I guess you could say — than most men. He was a friend of David's. I didn't mean to use him; it wasn't like that. I thought I really loved him, but those feelings I have for women didn't go away. Only recently have I realized that I loved Robert as a very close friend, not a lover." Lauren was crying. "You've attended classes at the academy. It's tough for new agents. Students develop tight relationships with their classmates that last long after they graduate, even after they leave the FBI. I became very close to a woman in the next suite. You know how the dorm rooms are, with a bathroom shared between two rooms. It became convenient after her roommate quit. We studied intensely, and you know what happened. I was her first lesbian relationship, and she was from a religious family. Between the pressures of the school and our relationship, she cracked and withdrew from the academy. Although there were suspicions, they had no definite proof."

Maris, quiet, listening, grabbed Lauren's hand and held it.

"Then Robert came up for the weekend, and we became engaged. I'm sure it helped that he took a job with the Justice Department as a U.S. attorney in Chicago. They decided that if anything really happened between us two girls, it was just an aberration, probably due to the isolation and pressure of the academy. After all, I couldn't possibly be gay and sleep with a man and, as I heard one idiot say, I was too pretty to be a dyke." Lauren took a ragged breath. "I survived and was assigned to Chicago where we married. Things went well for three and a half years until I met a woman, an accountant, who consulted with me on a case. It was bound to happen sooner or later. Then, disaster of all disasters, I got pregnant. One of those rare failures of birth control pills, because I was using antibiotics for a sinus infection that was slow to clear up. I didn't want a baby, I didn't want to interrupt my career, and I wanted to leave Robert for Diane. I got an abortion, which just about destroyed him and my family, after he so kindly called them and told them about it. We're all good Irish Catholics, you know. A lesbian and a baby-killer was just too much for them to handle, except for David, who stood by me. I insisted on a divorce, which Robert didn't want. He was very difficult until the final papers were signed, and I'm still not sure that my career is not in the toilet. Three months ago, Diane, my accountant, went back to her ex-lover. I tried to commit suicide, but David found me and pulled me out of it in time. I never even went to the doctor, so the Bureau never found out. The divorce was just recently final. I've always used my maiden name, so at least I didn't have to deal with that. I hadn't talked to anyone in the family, except David, for almost six months until Irene called to say Karin had disappeared."

"Lauren," Maris said softly.

"No, wait, Robert was the U.S. attorney on the bank robbery case. He should have excused himself, but he didn't. I think the bastard wanted a chance to make me miserable. I know you felt something was wrong, but it wasn't exactly the way you thought. I'm sorry I didn't tell you sooner, but I wasn't ready. It's hard to admit that your life is so screwed up. The leave of absence may have been timely for me and the Bureau, although I regret the reason. You're the only good thing that has happened to me in a long time, but, you have to admit, our future together is at best uncertain. I'm finished. What do you think about me now?"

Maris squeezed her tightly. "I'm in shock. I can't believe you're a lawyer. God, I never thought I'd sleep with a fucking lawyer."

Lauren punched her in the chest, and said angrily, "Damn you, Maris. I bare my soul to you, tell you my life story, and that's all you can say."

The punch hurt, and Maris rubbed her chest. "Lauren, I know we may have problems ahead. This is a hard time for you. I know our jobs can make it difficult. And God knows, I don't think I'm cut out for a long-distance romance, but on top of all that, I love you."

"Oh, Maris, I don't know if we have a chance, but I fell in love with you the first day I came here. You and that damned dog."

"For now, let's take it a day at a time. Earnhardt is particular about his women, and he's used to you. I guess I ought to keep you around as long as I can."

"It won't be much longer."

"I know, Lauren, I know," she said, but she wondered, what then? What then?

Chapter Fourteen

Up by seven o'clock despite the late hours, Maris poured David a cup of coffee at the breakfast bar and tried to hide her embarrassment. Responding to his gentle teasing, she soon relaxed. He told her that he was also gay and at odds with the family. It seemed to Maris that they had a very tight-assed and unforgiving family, but she didn't say anything. After a quick breakfast of cereal and milk, David read the paper while Lauren slept for another hour and Maris went to work.

She opened the laboratory and quickly worked

four drug cases. Two of the cases contained meth-
amphetamine, which seemed to be rivaling cocaine
once again as the drug of choice. At nine o'clock, she
stopped to work on the Karin Beauchamp evidence.
Lauren, dressed in dress slacks, a white silky blouse
and patterned vest, interrupted her with a knock on
the glass sliding door.

"We'll be in Pierce to help Irene with the funeral
arrangements," she said. "I'll call you later."

Maris kissed her and watched her walk away. She
waved at David and locked the door, returning to the
Beauchamp evidence. She went through her records
exhibit by exhibit to organize her thoughts. Her
attention fell on the photograph of the print on the
steering wheel. She held up both the original
photographs and the 1:1 blowups. Using a magnifying
glass, she studied the print in the Luminol and
amido-black-enhanced images. She hadn't been sure at
the scene, but it was clearly a thumbprint, a left
thumbprint. She held her thumb up to the enlarged
photograph and paused. Her thumb and the thumbprint in the photograph were approximately the same
size. She found a ruler and double-checked the scale.
There was no doubt about it, the thumbprint was
small, too small to be Bobby Joe Beauchamp's. Could
it be a woman or boy? Maris wasn't sure about the
size of Brian's hands, but she figured them to be
larger than her own.

She made notes until the phone rang. Wayne
Coffey said, "Maris, I have some news. Brian was
making the telephone calls to your house and Bennie
Wright's. Since he's a juvenile they had to let him
post bond and turned him over to his parents last
week after we charged him with assault."

"So he was out of jail when Bennie died."

"Yes, but it's Bobby Joe who did it. Back to Brian, the S.O. busted him on the telephone calls. Yesterday, when he heard we found Karin's body, he tore up the jail, banging his head against the wall and shouting, 'I did it. The beast was angry. I killed Karin.' The jailers thought he'd settled down and was doing okay when the idiot tried to hang himself. They found him before any serious damage was done. Now he's in the hospital."

"Brian is just not a normal young man, is he?" she commented. "So, do you believe him?"

"I don't know, but I wanted to call and ask if you have anything new. What about the tarp?"

"It's my opinion that this tarp was in the back of Bobby Joe's pickup. The cuts and tears in it match up to gaps in the stain." She explained the results of her examinations and told him about the wood fibers on the tarp. "Also, Wayne," she said, "I'm currently looking at a photo of a print on the steering wheel of the pickup. Unfortunately, there isn't enough detail to compare fingerprints even with the amido black for enhancement. It appears to be a left thumbprint. What surprised me was its size. It's small, about the size of my thumbprint. I don't think it could have come from Bobby Joe. I'm not sure about Brian. I didn't pay much attention to his hands, but judging from his height and weight, I don't think it's his. I suspect a female or younger boy made this print."

"Could you type the blood on the print?"

"No, it did respond positively to a preliminary test for blood, but there's not enough for anything else.

That steering wheel was wiped clean, but there was enough of the stain remaining to respond to the Luminol and the amido black."

"Do you think that Irene Beauchamp could pick up the body, wrap it in a tarp and move it by herself, Maris?"

"No, not Irene, not by herself. I'm bigger and stronger than she is, and I would have had difficulty moving her by myself."

"It's crossed my mind that we don't really know for sure that she stayed in bed all night long. Suppose she left after Bobby Joe passed out? Who else also has access to the truck?"

"Yes, but if she left, where did she go, and why?"

"I don't know. Guess who called me this morning to change her story?"

"Who?"

"Elaine, she now says Brian is the only one really interested in Satanic cults, but that the others tolerated it, and she sometimes dabbled in it with him. None of the kids took it seriously, except Brian. He even stole and sacrificed a goat. He convinced some of the kids to drink the blood by telling them it would give them incredible sexual prowess."

"Disgusting. I guess that's how the blood got onto Karin's blouse?"

"Probably, Elaine says that she was there. These parties were mainly acid and XTC parties. Brian has a source to buy the LSD papers and XTC tablets, and he sells them to the others. Elaine says that there is sex at the parties, but only between couples, no orgies. Karin had an affair with Bennie Wright,

139

but he hasn't attended any of these parties. He usually picked Karin up at the gate without entering the field."

"Bet he knew about the drugs and the underage drinking. What else did she say?"

"Karin was upset that Friday night because she suspected Bennie Wright was seeing someone else. Brian was pissed because she was moping around over Bennie. They were arguing when they left the party, and that's all Elaine knows."

"What does she say about the other Satanic cult rumors in Pierce? What about the day care center?"

"Oh, damn, I'm suspicious about those allegations. It seems that once some of this hit the papers everyone started seeing devil worshipers everywhere. Elaine doubted the story. Said she'd never seen any adults participate, but she supposed that Brian could have learned it at home. Her parents are contemplating sending her to live with relatives in Oklahoma City to get her life straightened out."

"Sounds like a good idea to me. What now?"

"It's time I had a talk with Mr. Beauchamp. We're waiting for the search warrant to look for bloodstained clothes and a pair of work boots with the wavy sole tread. I intend to ask him about the tarp. Maybe he'll break down and confess to killing both Bennie and Karin."

"See if you can get me a known blood sample from him. I'll try to extract spermatozoa from the stains on the panties that Lauren found in Karin's room and do DNA PCR. The results may confirm our theory of abuse. Karin may have threatened to turn him in on the sexual abuse charges. What if Bennie knew and threatened to go public with the charges?

I'll try to wrap up the analysis on this evidence within the next two weeks and send you a copy of the report."

Maris thought about Brian Blake as she put down the receiver. What turmoil must go through that boy's head? She was certain that Brian Blake was involved in Karin's death, either as the murderer or as a witness. His strange behavior during the interrogation combined with the Satanic activity and drug abuse was incriminating. She was anxious to hear about Wayne's conversation with Bobby Joe.

Starving, Maris broke for lunch, surprised that it was already three o'clock. Answering the phone after two rings, she failed initially to recognize Lauren's distressed voice. "Bobby Joe is dead, and Irene is in the hospital," she said.

"Dead?" Maris was shocked. "What happened?"

"When we arrived in Pierce about eleven this morning, we went to the S.O. to talk to Wayne Coffey and Ralph Lambert. They'd just received the search warrant for Bobby Joe when a nine-one-one call came in from Irene. We raced to the house and found Bobby Joe with a gunshot wound. According to Irene, she caught Bobby Joe burning a bloody shirt and some photographs in the fireplace. She confronted him, accusing him of murdering Bennie Wright. He came at her with the fireplace poker. She ran into the bedroom and grabbed a twenty-two caliber Beretta from her nightstand. She shot him once in the upper left thigh before he knocked the gun out of her hand with the fireplace poker and began to beat her. Maris," she said, pausing, "he would have beat her to death, but he had a heart attack and collapsed. The doctor said it wasn't the gunshot that killed him. Paramedics revived him once, but he died shortly after arrival in the emergency room."

"What about Irene?"

"They don't think she has a concussion, but she has several stitches along the top of her ear and side of her head. Most of the blow was downward. Her left wrist is broken and both arms are terribly bruised where she tried to ward him off. She'll be in the hospital overnight at least."

"Where are you now?"

"Pierce County Memorial. David's here with me. Wayne and Ralph are still at the house. I don't really care about Bobby Joe, but I feel sorry for my poor sister. She's exhausted and in pain and shock. She can't stop crying. Because of the head injury, they're cautious about the medication they can give her to calm her down."

"I'm coming to Pierce. Give me about two hours," Maris said before hanging up.

Maris found the telephone number for the Beauchamp house in her notes and dialed. Someone called Wayne to the telephone. "Damn, can you believe this mess?" he said.

"Not really. Does Irene's story hold up?"

"Seems to. He was trying to burn a shirt and a cardboard box full of photographs in the fireplace. The photographs got the worst of it. The shirt was only partially burned, and there are blood spatters on the sleeves. The photographs look like they were taken in Bennie's bedroom. We think he was clandestinely taking pictures of women as they undressed, and as they participated in various sex acts with him. Sorry bastard! Most of the pictures are

142

unrecognizable, but we'll see if the photo lab can restore them. Also, we found a pair of work boots in Bobby Joe's closet with a sole pattern like we saw at Bennie's."

"Did Bobby Joe have a history of heart trouble?"

"Yeah, he had a history, and you've seen him. It was probably just a matter of time, but lucky for Irene it happened when it did. I wish he hadn't died before he could answer some questions, damn it. When I leave here, I'm going to the hospital. I want to talk to Irene again, if she's well enough. I'd like to talk to Mr. Blake, but the little bastard's still under observation as a mental case. This fucking case is driving everyone crazy!"

"I'll see you at the hospital, and I'll bring the photograph of the left thumbprint from Bobby Joe's pickup. I want to compare it with Brian's thumb for size, and Irene's."

"Maybe we'll let them think we can compare the prints for the fingerprint pattern and not only for size. I'll wait for you there."

Maris fed Earnhardt and gave him fresh water before she left for Pierce. Still famished, she made do with a diet Big Red as she sped toward Pierce. Now, Lauren and Irene had two funerals to plan.

Chapter Fifteen

Before looking for the Ranger, Maris sought out Lauren and David. She found them in a curtained room in emergency. They stepped into the corridor, and Lauren hugged Maris tightly. Maris gently pushed her away and asked, "How's she doing?"

"Better, since the mild sedative took effect. They wanted to keep her in emergency for a while under observation. They'll move her upstairs after the orthopedic doctor sets her wrist."

"I'm glad she's doing better. I need to find

Wayne, but I'll be back soon," Maris said, trying to smile encouragingly.

She found Wayne drinking coffee at the nurses' station on the first floor. Thorough as always, he had a vacutainer of known blood from Bobby Joe and a fingerprint card with his prints. It was obvious that the thumbprint was not from Bobby Joe.

"Shall we proceed to visit the devil's child?" Wayne asked.

Maris grinned and said, "Yeah, but you better be careful, or Brian'll get your goat."

Wayne groaned. "I was right. This fucking case is driving everyone crazy."

Laughing, she followed him to the elevator, and they rode up to the second floor where they found a deputy guarding the door to Brian's room.

"What's he doing?" Wayne asked the bored deputy.

"Same fucking thing he always does, talks trash and watches television. I don't think there's anything wrong with him. He's working on an insanity defense. He's got some tape recorder that he keeps talking into and playing back. He's supposed to use it to listen to relaxation tapes, but he's not."

"I talked to the doctor a few minutes ago. He said that we could talk to Brian if we wanted, not that it is likely to do any good. All we really want is a thumbprint. Come in as a witness." Wayne pushed open the door.

Brian looked small and ashen. His eyes, blood-red due to vein damage from the attempt to hang himself in the jail, glowered at them like live coals.

Wayne strode up to the bed and said, "Brian, this

is Maris Middleton, a chemist from the crime lab. She found a thumbprint on the steering wheel of Bobby Joe Beauchamp's Dodge truck. We have your fingerprint cards at the jail, but it'll save us some time if you'll let us make a thumbprint here to compare to the one in the picture."

"The mark of the devil is blood and fire," Brian mumbled, his head rolling, but he allowed Wayne to grab his hand and roll the left thumb in ink before pressing it to the white card. "The head of the beast breathes fire and spews out fresh blood to mark the children of the ram," he continued as Wayne wiped the ink off of Brian's thumb.

He handed the card with the print to Maris. She examined it and went through the motions of comparing it to the photograph, but she already knew it was too big. She shook her head and shrugged at Wayne.

Startled when Brian shouted, she turned and saw him pointing at her as he screamed, "She who chooses to walk in the path of darkness shall not forsake the beast, or vengeance will be sure and swift. And the sinner will be cast down into a deep sulphurous pit. She who is the bride of the Devil shall not break the covenant formed in the blood of the goat, or the hand of Satan, in the form of the Ram, shall strike the sinner a deadly blow. There shall be a black mass to honor the faithful, and the mother of the harlot will be called upon to participate, and her blood will wash the altar free of her daughter's sin. Then the pain of the beast and his followers will be wiped away. God can't help you now, but the devil will."

"Jesus," Wayne said, "let's get out of here."

"God, he sends chills up my back. He may well be the Devil's child," Maris said, shuddering as if from a sudden chill. "Do you think he's trying to tell us something?"

"Who the hell knows? It could be the insane ramblings of a fool who has acid-fried his brain."

"I wish I had a recording of everything he said."

"The doctor doesn't think the little bastard is dangerous, but I wouldn't be surprised to find out that boy was capable of anything. I'll be glad when they finally get him transferred somewhere with a real mental ward where they can lock up the little fucker. This hospital isn't very secure." As they waited for the elevator, Wayne said, "Maris, I keep thinking about some of the information we've been given in this case. It's apparent, I think, that Karin was not the victim of a sex crime. She was not kidnapped and raped by the Blakes or anyone else, but the foster girl hasn't changed her story. Could we have another missing girl?"

"Lord, I hope not. It's hard to evaluate the testimony of an abused, emotionally disturbed child. I hope the talk of Satan worship in this county is overblown, and Brian's talk is just drug-induced psychosis. What's next?"

"I think I'm going to take the partially burned photographs from the Beauchamp house and study them. Maybe they'll turn up something."

"Could Bennie have helped Irene move the body?"

"I don't know. Damn it, Maris, why would she kill her daughter? Surely not for Bennie Wright, or to protect Bobby Joe."

"I've been thinking about all of the hit and runs that I've worked. They all seem to have three things

147

in common — people don't stop because they're drunk or on drugs, or they're carrying contraband they don't want the police to know about, or they're somewhere they're not supposed to be, doing something they're not supposed to be doing. What if Irene ran over her and killed her accidentally?"

"I thought about that. It's dark out on that highway. What if Brian brought Karin back and dropped her off? And someone was coming home at the same time she crossed the highway? Karin may have been drinking, or using drugs. She was upset and may not have been careful crossing the highway. There was an accident, and she was badly injured. Irene and whoever helped her carry the body probably thought Karin was dead." They rode the elevator to the first floor, and Wayne said, "Assuming we're right, who helped Irene move the body?"

"It keeps coming back to that question. The size of the thumbprint won't prove that Irene drove the pickup. When it gets right down to it, all I can prove is that the front end of the Dodge pickup probably came into contact with Karin, and she was wrapped in a tarp and carried in the back of the Dodge pickup. The tarp appears to have come from the Beauchamps' woodpile. It's all circumstantial, and even at that, it's weak. If a witness doesn't come forward, or she doesn't break and confess, I don't know if we can ever prove anything, Wayne."

"We can't make an arrest until we have more evidence, or we find the person who helped her move the body. If it's Bobby Joe or Bennie Wright, we've got a problem, but I've seen some strange things happen to break a case. Irene's conscience could get to her."

Irene was still in the observation room in emergency, and Lauren met them at the door. "We're still waiting. The doctor hasn't gotten here to set her wrist yet."

Wayne said, "I wanted to talk to her, but it sounds like I need to wait until tomorrow. Oh, hell, that's my pager going off. A Ranger's work is never done." He grinned, leaving with a wave. They watched as he strode purposefully down the hall, his boots echoing off of the waxed tile.

Maris, her stomach growling furiously, persuaded Lauren to go eat. David agreed to stay with Irene and wait for the doctor. He wanted to be there if they moved Irene to her room. Maris promised to bring him back something good for supper.

The truck stop was the only thing open after seven o'clock, except for the Dairy Queen. Lauren rode silently, lost in her own thoughts, and Maris did not push her to talk.

As Maris turned into the truck stop, Lauren said, "I've been thinking about this all day. She did it. I know she did it." She burst into tears as Maris parked the pickup.

Maris slid across the seat and held her tightly, stroking her hair. After several more minutes, her crying eased, except for the occasional sob. Maris found two napkins in the glove compartment and handed them to Lauren.

"I'm right, aren't I? She did it."

"Wayne and I think so, but it may have been an accident. Someone had to help her move the body. I know she couldn't have done it by herself."

"An accident doesn't excuse throwing your daughter down a well. Why would she do it? I keep

149

running it through my mind, and I can't conceive of any reason why a mother would murder her daughter or, if it was an accident, not do everything to help her. Maternal instinct should take over. To think she condemned me for an abortion."

When Lauren was better, they entered the truck stop and slid into a corner booth. After a tired waitress took their orders, Lauren went to call David and check on Irene. She removed a scrap of paper from her purse and scooted out of the red vinyl booth.

She returned shortly and said, "The doctor finally got there and put a cast on her wrist. They moved her to the second floor, room two-fifteen. David says there's a deputy up there. Surely they don't think she's a flight risk?"

"No, he's up there to guard Brian. That boy is a crazy son-of-a-bitch. He was arrested again for making the threatening phone calls to me and Bennie Wright. When he was told they found Karin's body, he went wild. Before they could do anything he tried to hang himself and had to be hospitalized. You should have heard some of his ramblings this afternoon."

The waitress arrived with a club sandwich for Lauren and a huge chicken-fried steak next to a mountain of mashed potatoes, both smothered in cream gravy, for Maris. She was ravenous. Lauren picked at her french fries and sandwich while Maris attacked her food with relish, devouring it quickly.

After a gulp of iced tea, she said, "Brian said some crazy things today." She shifted her weight and removed a small notebook and pen from her back pocket. As Lauren watched, she wrote down Brian's wild speech as she remembered it. "Here," she said, handing the notebook across the table. "What do you think of this? He pointed directly at me when he said it."

"At first glance it seems to be ramblings, but sometimes these rantings have a hidden meaning. 'Forsaken,' 'bride of the devil,' 'covenant of goat's blood,' could possibly refer to his relationship with Karin and his feelings of betrayal."

"I suppose. It just doesn't make much sense. 'The hand of Satan in the form of the Ram will strike the sinner down,' or something to that effect. I don't know." She shrugged. The truth hit her like a sledge-hammer, and her full stomach cramped painfully.

"Maris, Maris, what is it?" Lauren said, reaching across the table to touch Maris's arm.

"Oh, my God, 'in the form of the Ram.' The Dodge pickup is called a Ram. It has the emblem of a ram's head on the front of the hood. We've got to go back to the hospital, now. Damn, I can't believe we let them put her on the same floor with that crazy bastard. We'll call from the car phone." Maris tried to calm herself. Everything should be fine. David was there to watch Irene, and the deputy was there to watch Brian.

Lauren stared at the notebook, trying to decipher the message and Maris's urgency. " 'The mother of the whore will participate, and her blood will wash free her daughter's sins,' " she read. Looking up, she said, "He means my sister. He wants to sacrifice my sister."

Maris threw the money on the table, and they ran from the restaurant. As they approached the pickup, Maris asked, "Do you have a gun?"

"No, since I'm on leave officially, they told me not to travel with my gun."

"Shit, take this one," Maris said as she opened the door of the pickup and grabbed a zippered gun bag from under the seat. "It's my thirty-eight Smith and Wesson, and it's loaded."

Maris drove and called out Wayne's number from memory to Lauren, who dialed furiously on the car phone. She reached his answering machine and left a frantic message telling him they were worried about Irene and had figured out Brian's crazy talk at the hospital. Wayne would think they were both crazy, Maris thought, if they rushed to the hospital and found everyone sleeping peacefully.

"Call the S.O. and have them check on the deputy," Maris said.

"Good idea, I should have thought of that," Lauren said as she called directory assistance. They were halfway to the hospital when Lauren finally reached the deputy in charge of the night shift, a sergeant. She quickly explained the situation to him, and he told her to hold while he attempted to contact the deputy on his handheld radio.

Within minutes, the Sergeant returned to the telephone and said, "We can't get him on the radio, and the PD's running on a nine-one-one call from the hospital. Got to go!"

Lauren clung to the seat and helped Maris watch for traffic as they raced through the empty streets of Pierce. She slammed on the brakes as they crossed Main Street. With tires squealing, she turned a corner sideways, straightened the truck and accelerated down a short street. They traveled the remaining two short blocks to the hospital fast enough to win the admiration of any ambulance driver. When they shot into the parking lot, they saw one city police car and two county cars, all with lights flashing. The truck screeched to a halt. They vaulted out, leaving the doors open and ran into the hospital. Taking two steps at a time, they soon reached the second floor. Gasping for air, they stopped and carefully opened the door. A clock on the wall behind the nurses' station told them it was a quarter to nine.

To get to Brian's room, they had to pass the nurses' station and turn right at the corner. The waiting room was on the left after they turned the corner, if Maris remembered correctly, and Brian's room was several doors down on the right side of the same hallway. She thought from the room number that Irene's room would be close to Brian's. Keeping low, they ran to the corner, stopping for Lauren, in the lead, to peer down the hall. On tiptoe, Maris looked around her and saw a police officer and two deputies in the waiting room bent over someone slumped in a chair. When one of the deputies moved, Maris and Lauren saw that the injured person was David. An officer held a towel to his wounded shoulder, but rapidly spreading blood soon soaked it.

Lauren gasped, and one of the deputies looked back at her. He held up his hand, told her to stay where she was, and formed his other hand in an imaginary receiver. He disappeared from the doorway, and in a few seconds the telephone on the nurses' station rang. Maris jerked it from its cradle, and Lauren moved to stand nearby.

Maris identified herself. "I'm working for Lauren O'Conner, his sister. She's FBI and standing here with me," she said. "How's he doing, and what happened?"

"I'm Steven Hobbs, S.O., and he'll be fine. He was slashed by a piece of broken mirror that Brian Blake used as a weapon. Brian also hurt our deputy pretty bad, but the nurses managed to get him out of the hallway and downstairs to the emergency room. Brian's now cornered in Irene Beauchamps' room. He's got the deputy's gun."

"What about Irene?"

"We're not sure. Our boys are across the hall and on each side of the Irene's room, but he's moved her bed away from the door. We can't see either one of them."

"We're going to move over where you are," Maris said. "I want to be where I can hear radio communications."

"Be careful crossing the hall. He fired a couple of shots at one of the other deputies."

They crossed over one at a time without incident. David said, "Sorry, Lauren, I didn't do much good. I heard the deputy scream and ran down the hall. Brian had a piece of broken mirror. I rushed him, but he slashed my arm. I tried to stop him as he bent over to grab the deputy's gun, but he was too quick. He cut my wrist and ran into Irene's room."

"David did great," Steven said. "He and a nurse pulled the deputy to safety. Brian fired two shots at them but luckily missed. The deputy would have bled to death if they hadn't moved him when they did. The nurses took him down to emergency. They'll be coming for David soon."

"I should have stopped him," he said, looking at Lauren.

She nodded. "You did all you could." She started to say something else when they were all startled by the large figure of Texas Ranger Wayne Coffey as he hurtled into the room.

"I knew that little fucker would be trouble," he said. He listened quietly while the deputy explained the tactical situation. They could hear the other officers down the hallway talking to Brian, pleading for him to surrender. His replies were nonsense.

"Has he hurt her?" Wayne asked.

"We don't really know. He keeps saying something about her being in purgatory already," Steven said. "We were thinking about using tear gas, but we can't move most of the patients, and the nurses informed us many of the patients will be adversely affected with just a small amount of the gas."

"Don't want to use that, then. I reckon I'll just have to go down there and get the little bastard out." He checked his gun and was gone before anyone could say anything. Maris leaned around the door and was amused to see him walking down the middle of the hallway. That crazy bastard, she thought, he's showing off for the FBI. She looked over at Lauren and grinned.

Lauren whispered, "What the hell is he doing?"

"He's showing you and the FBI how the Rangers handle a situation."

"Well, I hope he doesn't get his ass shot off."

"Don't worry. The devil himself wouldn't dare shoot Texas Ranger Wayne Coffey."

"Brian Blake," they heard Wayne say, "you sorry little motherfucker. I'm going to come in there and get you. I'm all the devil you need to worry about."

They all watched in amazement as Wayne strode

into the room without missing a step. Everyone was silent, fearing the noise of a shot, but nothing happened. Almost as quickly as he entered, the Ranger returned to the hallway.

"He's gone, and he took Irene with him. Those rantings are from this tape recorder. Damn it!" He handed the recorder to a stunned deputy.

Chapter Sixteen

"He's going to sacrifice her," Maris said. "He told us this afternoon when we were in his room, but it took me a while to decipher his message. He saw Irene run over Karin with the Dodge Ram. In his twisted mind the truck was the devil's instrument to punish Karin for screwing around with Bennie, but he also blames Irene. Therefore, using his logic, Irene must be sacrificed to the Devil to make amends."

"He'll take her back to the clearing with the stone wall and the altar," Wayne said, already running to the elevator with Lauren close behind.

"He won't go there," Maris said. "He thinks we desecrated it during the search."

"But where else would he go?" Lauren asked.

Steven Hobbs jammed the closing doors with his elbow and jumped onto the elevator. "They called from downstairs. Brian was seen half carrying and half dragging an unconscious woman. He used the fire escape to get to the parking lot, pushed a woman out of her car and took off with it. It's a red Chevrolet."

"Radio Ralph Lambert. He's on his way here. Tell him to get to the clearing we searched," Wayne told him as the doors opened on the ground floor.

Wayne and Lauren ran to the Ranger's Chevrolet Caprice. Maris started to follow, but stopped in her tracks. She knew that Brian would not go to the clearing with the altar and the stone wall. If not, where would he go? Wayne's Chevrolet flashed by with two sheriff's department cars close behind. Heading slowly to her truck, Maris knew time was short, but it wouldn't matter if she didn't know where to go. Brian would avoid the clearing at Devil's Leg Crossing for the same reason he wouldn't use the altar at the stone wall. But what about the hanging tree? It had a history of violence and death. She ran to the truck.

It felt right. He'd go to Devil's Leg Crossing, to the giant oak that served as the hanging tree. There, under the magnificent branches, he'd kill Irene. She picked up the mobile phone and called the sheriff's office. She told them to contact Wayne Coffey and tell him to go to Devil's Leg Crossing, even though she knew Wayne would go to the altar first.

Near the crossing, she cut the headlights on the Ford truck and slowed to a crawl. Lauren had her gun, but Maris kept an ax handle behind the seat of the truck. Once evidence in a vicious assault case, it had a hole drilled in one end with a leather strap tied through it. Maris kept it when the case was closed and they'd had permission to dispose of the evidence.

Stopping several yards from the crossing, she got the ax handle from behind the seat, softly closed the door and trotted toward the hanging tree. She saw the red Chevrolet nearby, its headlights shining on the concrete picnic table. Irene, nude except for the fresh white cast on her left wrist, was tied spread-eagle to the table. Brian, clad in a purple robe, loomed over her chest, clutching a shiny stainless steel dagger. Eyes closed, he ceremonially chanted something Maris could not understand. She assumed Brian had retrieved the robe and dagger from a hiding place that she and Lauren missed when they found the goat.

She crept up to the side of the Chevrolet until she reached the front quarter panel. She hoped the glare from the headlights would make it difficult for him to see her clearly. "Brian," she yelled, "you don't want to do this."

"Come forth sinner and show thyself," he shouted as he lowered the dagger and stood looking toward her.

"Throw the knife over here, and we'll talk about it."

"There's nothing to talk about. She must die." He raised the dagger over his head.

"No," Maris shouted. "You're making a mistake. As a juvenile, you can still get out of this without a lengthy sentence. You can't if you murder Irene."

"You don't understand. I must obey the commands of the Master. She must die."

"For killing Karin?"

"The Ram killed Karin. She had to be punished. She was the devil's bride, but she was unfaithful."

"You were there and helped Irene move Karin's body to the well?" Maris asked.

"The mother was unfaithful with the same demon and demanded secrecy, but the Dark One wants blood for blood." Closing his eyes, he resumed the unintelligible chanting. Hoping to avoid detection by Brian, she stepped out into the light and inched toward the table.

Brian's arms tensed and his voice rose. Anticipating the plunge of the dagger, Maris rushed the concrete table and sprang up on the first bench seat. Using the ax handle as a battering ram, she slammed the end of the handle square into Brian's chest. He yelped in pain and toppled backwards, lost in the shadows on the other side of the table. Stepping over Irene, Maris saw her moan and pull weakly at the ropes. Dropping to the ground, she didn't find Brian where she expected, and she squinted into the darkness.

Her eyes gradually adjusted from the bright light of the headlights to the darkness as she stood poised with the ax handle and waited. She heard a movement to her right and leapt forward. Jerking her head away, she felt a sharp burning sensation down her right cheek and the side of her neck. Frantically, she swung the handle as hard as she could. She felt a satisfying vibration up the varnished wooden handle and heard Brian groan and fall to the ground. She stumbled over a rock, or stick, and went down on one knee. In the shadows, she could see him struggling to regain his footing. She stood and, without mercy, violently swung the ax handle. This time, she caught him in the forehead, and his head snapped back with a sickening crack. He fell, flinging his arms outward, and landed solidly on his back.

In the shadow of the picnic table, Maris waited warily. He made no attempt to rise, and she wondered vaguely if she'd killed him. She tripped on the dagger when she stepped toward the picnic table. Stooping down, she felt something warm and sticky running into the corner of her right eye. Puzzled, she stumbled around the picnic table into the light from the car. Thinking that she was sweating heavily, she touched her cheek and was annoyed to see blood when she studied her fingers in the light from the car. Wiping the blood on her jeans, she used the dagger to cut the ropes holding Irene. For the first time, she noticed a fresh bruise with slight bleeding on Irene's forehead. Irene pulled against the ropes and mumbled something. Maris, worried about a second head injury, hesitated to leave her alone, even briefly, but her face was beginning to sting, and she worried that Irene would go deeper into shock.

With the ax handle tucked under her arm, Maris ran to her truck, pausing only to shake her head and brush the blood away. She drove the pickup over to the picnic table. Irene and Brian hadn't moved, and she wondered again if Brian was dead. She grabbed an orange blanket from the camper of the pickup. After untying the rope, she helped Irene sit up on the edge of the table, then wrapped the blanket around her.

"You'll be fine," Maris said, wiping her cheek with a corner of the blanket. "Help will be here soon."

Irene didn't respond. Maris heard the sound of vehicles rapidly approaching. She waited patiently, holding the ax handle in her left hand and supporting Irene with her right. They were quickly surrounded with a flood of light as Wayne, the deputies and Lauren rushed over. Maris smelled hot oil and water from the police vehicles and heard a radiator hissing.

"He's over there," Maris said, pointing to the other side of the table. "I don't know if he's dead or alive."

"He's breathing, barely," Ralph Lambert said as he bent over Brian's prone figure.

"You're hurt," Lauren said, touching Maris's cheek. Wayne handed her his handkerchief, and Lauren pressed it against Maris's cut cheek and neck. It was soon saturated with blood.

"I've got two ambulances on the way," a deputy called from one of the cars.

Maris didn't realize she was weak until she tried to stand. Lauren protested, but it was the dizziness, not Lauren, that forced her down on the table. She briefly described to Lauren and Wayne what had happened and how she knew where to find Brian.

"He must be a hard-headed son-of-a-bitch to survive a blow from that," Wayne said, gesturing to the ax handle.

"I was afraid he still had the deputy's gun, but all he had was the dagger."

"The gun's here in the car," a deputy said from the open door of the red Chevrolet.

Maris shook her head slightly. "Brian said, 'She was seeing the same demon as Karin,' or something to that effect."

"The same demon?" Wayne asked.

"I think he meant Bennie Wright. Irene was driving the Dodge truck to meet Bennie when the store clerk saw it for the second time on the night Karin disappeared. She was coming back from Bennie's place when she accidentally hit her daughter. Brian was with Karin, bringing her home. He helped Irene hide the body. I don't understand why they felt that they couldn't simply get help for her and call it an accident. Guess she didn't want Bobby Joe to know where she'd been."

Two ambulances arrived simultaneously, and four paramedics sprang into action. They carefully placed Brian on a stretcher and loaded him into one of the ambulances. Maris refused help until the paramedics had taken Irene by stretcher to the second ambulance. Stubbornly, she insisted on walking to the ambulance but gallantly accepted assistance negotiating the step from a pretty paramedic with a tight uniform shirt. Lauren drove Maris's truck back to the hospital.

Worried about the cut on Maris's cheek, for cosmetic reasons and the possibility of nerve damage, the hospital called in a plastic surgeon to suture it. The cut started slightly behind the corner of the right eye and extended straight down to the end of her jaw. When she jerked her head, the knife had skipped, or bounced, and the tip stabbed her in the neck. The neck wound was minor, taking only two or three stitches.

David, nearly forty stitches in his wrist and shoulder, waited in emergency for Lauren and Maris to return and take him home. Irene was conscious and could answer simple questions, but they were concerned about the second head injury so soon after the first. She was placed under close observation not far from Brian, who was in guarded condition. He was unconscious for over two hours and X-rays revealed a hairline skull fracture. The doctor briefly considered keeping Maris overnight, but she insisted on going home. The doctor, too tired to argue, finally said, "To hell with it, give her some pain medicine and let her go."

Lauren borrowed cleaning supplies from the hospital to clean the blood out of Maris's pickup.

"The doctors think Brian'll be all right. No permanent brain damage," he said as he helped Maris into the truck.

"How the hell can they tell, as crazy as that bastard is?" Maris asked as she slid to the middle of the front bench seat. Lauren jumped in the driver's side.

"Good question. Are you sure you want to go home, Maris?" he asked, fastening David's seat belt for him.

"I'd rather hurt at home than here."

"You sound like a Ranger." Leaning into the truck across David's lap, he said to Lauren, "I'll have a deputy at the door to Irene's hospital room. We won't take her to jail until the doctor says she can go. I'm sorry it turned out like it did."

"I don't understand her, but she is my sister."

"I know, and if I were you, I'd convince her to cut a deal with the district attorney. She'll have to do some time, but she doesn't want to face a jury trial, not in this county. A mother who throws her injured daughter down a well — they'll hit her with everything they can."

Lauren sighed. "Wayne, she deserves some time for this. I want her to do some time, but I won't abandon her. I'll talk to you tomorrow. I'll have to do something about my rental car. Maris didn't want to leave her truck here because of all the equipment stored in the back."

"Fine, I'll keep you informed," he said, stepping back to close the truck door. "You two casualties take care. Maris, don't be drinking any whiskey with those pain pills."

"Why the hell do you think I wanted to go home tonight?" Maris said. Wayne laughed and walked away after carefully closing the pickup door.

Trying not to clench her teeth and tighten the muscles in her cheek, Maris rode silently. She was already hurting, and they hadn't even reached the highway. David, pale and silent, seemed to be hurting even worse. She put her hand on Lauren's thigh, squeezing it affectionately. At least she had a pretty nurse.

Chapter Seventeen

Released from the hospital on Friday morning, Irene, with Lauren and Maris for escorts, reported directly to the sheriff's office. There, haggard but calm, Irene accepted a cup of coffee and told her story in a soft, emotionless voice, her gaze rarely rising from the table.

Maris and Lauren watched from the observation room. There were dark circles under Lauren's eyes, and her pale color told of the strain on her. A fresh bandage covered the cut on Maris's right cheek, but there was no permanent muscle or nerve damage and, despite her worries, her dimple had appeared, intact, when she grinned at the mirror that morning. Maris draped an arm around Lauren's shoulders as they listened to Irene's tale.

After Bobby Joe had passed out, Irene hurried to Bennie's trailer, driving the Dodge truck, which was parked behind her car. She had sex with Bennie and was leaving when he played the messages on his answering machine. She heard a shocking message from Karin — a message that left no doubt that she also was intimate with Bennie. He laughed, bragged about it. She ran from the trailer, furious at Bennie and Karin.

It happened so fast, Irene told her solemn audience. She saw Karin and Brian on the side of the road and jerked her foot off the accelerator, but she was already nearly even with them. Before she could hit the brakes, Karin was in front of the truck, and Irene couldn't stop or swerve in time. She couldn't be sure, but when she thought about it afterwards, she thought Brian pushed Karin into the truck's path. Horrified, she stopped.

Brian, already bending over Karin when Irene reached her, screamed, "We murdered her!" She attempted to calm him down and check on Karin, but he shouted, "They'll know you killed her on purpose — to get Bennie. When Bobby Joe finds out, he'll kill you and Bennie."

She panicked and begged Brian to help her hide the body. She thought Karin was dead. It wasn't supposed to end this way, she said. She married Bobby Joe because she loved him and needed him. She stayed because he provided well for her and Karin. She confronted him once about his sexual abuse of Karin, but he denied it and threatened to kill them both if she spread rumors about him to anyone. She knew he was lying, and she kept a pair of Karin's bloodstained panties for proof, but she could never bring herself to report the abuse. The doctors told Bobby Joe four years ago that he would die of a heart attack if he didn't stop smoking and drinking and lose seventy-five pounds. He refused to change. She and Karin had suffered too much to leave and give up the money. After he died, she planned to use the money to make everything up to Karin. Killing Karin was an accident, but once it was done, she couldn't lose both Karin and the money. They had earned that money. She felt she had no choice but to cover up the accident.

"She knew about the abuse. She knew about it and allowed it to continue," Lauren said. "There is not enough money in the world to justify allowing that to happen. How could a mother do that?"

Maris was grieved to hear the hurt in her voice. "I don't know," she said. "Maybe she was really afraid of him, maybe not. She's not the first mother to prostitute her child for security. Maybe, subconsciously, she was resentful over Karin's relationship with Bennie."

"I don't think I can ever forgive her."

"Some things are unforgivable."

They were silent as Irene continued with her story. Although she had heard rumors that Bobby Joe was a suspect in Bennie's murder, she didn't really believe it until she came home unexpectedly and caught him burning his shirt and the photographs. She guessed that Bobby Joe found the pictures when he searched for Bennie's gun-cleaning supplies to

168

stage the suicide. The photographs shocked her. She hadn't known they existed. She didn't think there were any of her, or he would have killed her on the same day he killed Bennie.

Irene's attorney, in the presence of Wayne and Ralph, called the district attorney. He seemed agreeable to a plea bargain but wanted to wait until all of the reports and lab results were available — in order to make an informed decision. She was looking at ten years for vehicular homicide but would actually only serve about three. There would be no charges filed in Bobby Joe's death.

Ten years is not long enough, Maris thought, for killing a pretty girl with a troubled childhood, a girl who was left to die alone in the bottom of a deep, damp, dark well by her own mother and a boy who supposedly loved her. It left her cold.

Lauren made both funeral arrangements for Sunday, two days after Irene's arrest, and after encouragement from Maris and David, she called her parents. They drove up from Fredericksburg for the funerals, barely spoke to their three children, ignored Maris completely and left without telling anyone good-bye.

Before David returned to Chicago, he and Lauren made arrangements for Irene's house to be closed for an extended period. Other decisions would be made after Bobby Joe's estate was probated. With the assets tied up, Irene couldn't make bail and remained in jail. Her time served would apply toward her prison sentence when formalities were completed on the plea bargain. David left on Tuesday, still in pain from his injuries.

Brian Blake recovered from his head injury with

at least as many of his faculties present as before, according to Wayne Coffey. Wayne predicted that Brian would be declared mentally unstable and, despite the serious charges against him, go to the mental hospital in Wichita Falls, or to a juvenile facility until he was eighteen.

As each loose end fell into place, Maris felt a growing unease. Each day, each hour and each minute brought closer the time when Lauren would return to Chicago. They discussed the situation over and over, but like a difficult algebra problem, the answer came out the same. Both were surprised at the intensity of their feelings for the other after such a short relationship, but it didn't make the decisions any easier. Maris had too much money invested in her new business to walk away, although she could probably get a job with the city of Chicago or the state of Illinois. On the other hand, Lauren still wanted to be an FBI agent. It was too hard, even now, for a woman to reach that level in law enforcement, and Maris couldn't ask her to give it up.

On the second Sunday in October, two weeks after Irene's arrest, with her business concluded in Pierce, Lauren boarded a Boeing 727 and left for Chicago. They'd been together for only four weeks. At first, they talked on the telephone regularly, but with their problems unchanged and no future plans to make, the conversations became more and more polite and awkward. Lauren had no vacation time to travel and very little free cash after her leave without pay.

Maris had no time and no money. The business, gaining a foothold but still struggling, took all that she had of both. She's slipping away, Maris realized, but didn't know what to do to stop it. She felt as lost, again, as she was after Mary Ann's death. She threw herself into completing the analysis of the Beauchamp evidence and catching up on her other cases. The PCR DNA results were as expected and corroborated most of Irene's story, as did the results of the fiber comparisons on the tarp and Karin's clothing.

It was the week before Thanksgiving — her first Thanksgiving without Mary Ann — and about five weeks after Lauren's return to Chicago when Kathy called and insisted that Maris join a team to play flag football in an AIDS benefit tournament sponsored by the bars and spread out over three Sundays. Maris balked at first, but finally agreed when Kathy explained they were in the thirty-and-over league and promised Maris that she could play quarterback. The games would start the first Sunday after Thanksgiving and finish a week before Christmas.

God, how Maris dreaded Christmas. She dreaded Thanksgiving too, but that fear was dulled by the overwhelming threat of Christmas. Holidays had always depressed her, yet last year, she still had Mary Ann. She wished there was some way to go to sleep and not wake up until New Year's Day.

Since there was not, she spent Thanksgiving Day with her parents at her sister's house in Austin. Everyone tried too hard to be cheerful, and her Mother fretted too much over the scar on Maris's cheek. Maris escaped on Friday to spend the night getting drunk and dancing with friends in Austin. She drove home Saturday with a throbbing headache, wishing that Earnhardt could drive.

Nervous before the first football game, Maris discovered that, despite Kathy's promise, she was really quarterback by default since she was the only one on the team who could throw a decent spiral over thirty yards. She and Lynn, who had only average speed but long arms and good hands, made quite a pair, just like Young and Rice.

Maris called Lauren after each game and finally admitted to her that the games were really organized beer busts. The games left her in a good mood until she and Lauren said good-bye. Then, the depression hit. She had not bought any Christmas presents or put up a single decoration. Except for the football games, all she did was work. Something had to change.

They were tied for first place going into the final game. The December sun was shining brightly, and the temperature was expected to be in the mid-sixties by game time, three o'clock. The unusually warm and dry fall weather was extending into the winter.

The game was tied at the two-minute mark in the fourth quarter. Ronnie, dark-headed and very attractive, intercepted a pass and gave Maris's team the ball on their opponent's twenty-two yard line. Kathy, faster than she should be on such short legs, ran the ball to the eleven for another first down. Maris missed Lynn in the end zone on the first down, narrowly avoiding an interception. They ran the ball on the second down to the five yard line. On third down, Lynn ran a crossing pattern across the middle, and Maris felt like Troy Aikman when she threw a bullet straight into Lynn's arms. They won the game and first place. Naturally, everyone was excited and in the mood to party.

"The Cowboys are on TNT tonight, their last Sunday night game this year," Kathy said. "Hope they do as good as we did."

"I don't know," Ronnie said. "Is their quarterback as good as ours?"

Trying not to show her pleasure at the remark, Maris said, "I hope they're not drinking as much beer as we are."

Ronnie turned thirty just two weeks before the tournament started, barely making the age requirement. Maris caught herself looking forward to seeing her every week and Ronnie seemed to feel the same way about her. When Ronnie moved closer to Maris and suggested a football party, Maris, temporarily spellbound, invited everyone over to her house to watch the game. They quickly organized into scouting parties with assignments to buy the makings for hamburgers and more beer. Maris's job was to go home, light the grill and turn on the television. Guiltily, she realized how excited she was at the opportunity to spend more time with Ronnie.

"Maris, I'll come with you and help get things ready," Kathy announced, breaking into her thoughts. "And this is your perfect opportunity to let me drive the convertible. You promised to let me."

Maris groaned, but it was true. She did promise to let Kathy drive the Olds 442, even if Kathy was the single worst driver she'd ever seen. "I was obviously drunk at the time and shouldn't be held accountable, but I'll keep my word. You can drive."

Kathy only made her cuss and slam on an

imaginary brake three times from the park to her house forty-five minutes away. When the house came into sight, Maris was surprised to see a car in the driveway behind the Ford pickup. She didn't recognize the car, a Honda Accord, when Kathy turned into the driveway and slammed on the brakes.

"Maris, I think you have a redhead sitting on your porch," Kathy said.

"I think you're right." Maris pushed the garage door opener and jumped out over the door of the car. "Go ahead and put her up."

"Boy, are you brave," Kathy said as she dropped into first gear.

Maris forced herself not to run as she cut in front of the truck and found her way to the porch. Lauren stood, waiting with her hands in her back pockets. She smiled. "Hello, stranger."

"Hello, yourself," Maris said, embracing her. Her heart pounded and she frowned, using all of her concentration to hold onto the house key. Ronnie didn't make her feel like this. "I can't believe you're really here. How did you arrange it?"

"I transferred to the Dallas bureau. The position came open suddenly, and I grabbed it. I hope you still want me, because here I am."

"Still want you? You're damned right I still want you. I just wish I hadn't invited a whole football team over to watch the Cowboys and eat supper." Maris opened the door and followed Lauren inside.

"Well, maybe they won't have extra innings," Lauren said as Maris disengaged the burglar alarm. "Your scar makes you even better looking," she added, running a long, dark red fingernail down Maris's cheek.

Maris bent to kiss her and Lauren greeted her passionately, her lips opening in welcome. Maris felt breasts rise and fall rapidly against her as her pulse accelerated. Kathy interrupted their reunion by pounding insistently on the door from the garage. Earnhardt barked furiously from the backyard, and Ronnie's red Blazer, full of women, roared into the driveway out front.

"You mean sudden death. Extra innings are in baseball." Maris laughed. "And it'll be the death of me if I have to wait for more than four quarters to take you to bed. You let the ladies in, and I'll rescue Kathy . . . and Earnhardt. He knows you're here."

As she stepped into the living room, Maris turned and said, "I love you, Lauren. Welcome home!"

BABY, IT'S COLD by Jaye Maiman. 256 pp. 5th Robin Miller
Mystery. ISBN 1-56280-141-4 19.95

WILD THINGS by Karin Kallmaker. 240 pp. By the undisputed
mistress of lesbian romance. ISBN 1-56280-139-2 10.95

THE GIRL NEXT DOOR by Mindy Kaplan. 208 pp. Just what
you'd expect. ISBN 1-56280-140-6 11.95

NOW AND THEN by Penny Hayes. 240 pp. Romance on the
westward journey. ISBN 1-56280-121-X 11.95

HEART ON FIRE by Diana Simmonds. 176 pp. The romantic and
erotic rival of Curious Wine. ISBN 1-56280-152-X 11.95

DEATH AT LAVENDER BAY by Lauren Wright Douglas. 208 pp.
1st Allison O'Neil Mystery. ISBN 1-56280-085-X 11.95

YES I SAID YES I WILL by Judith McDaniel. 272 pp. Hot
romance by famous author. ISBN 1-56280-138-4 11.95

FORBIDDEN FIRES by Margaret C. Anderson. Edited by Mathilda
Hills. 176 pp. Famous author's "unpublished" Lesbian romance.
ISBN 1-56280-123-6 21.95

SIDE TRACKS by Teresa Stores. 160 pp. Gender-bending
Lesbians on the road. ISBN 1-56280-122-8 10.95

HOODED MURDER by Annette Van Dyke. 176 pp. 1st Jessie
Batelle Mystery. ISBN 1-56280-134-1 10.95

WILDWOOD FLOWERS by Julia Watts. 208 pp. Hilarious and
heart-warming tale of true love. ISBN 1-56280-127-9 10.95

NEVER SAY NEVER by Linda Hill. 224 pp. Rule #1: Never get involved
with . . . ISBN 1-56280-126-0 10.95

THE SEARCH by Melanie McAllester. 240 pp. Exciting top cop
Tenny Mendoza case. ISBN 1-56280-150-3 10.95

THE WISH LIST by Saxon Bennett. 192 pp. Romance through
the years. ISBN 1-56280-125-2 10.95

FIRST IMPRESSIONS by Kate Calloway. 208 pp. P.I. Cassidy
James' first case. ISBN 1-56280-133-3 10.95

OUT OF THE NIGHT by Kris Bruyer. 192 pp. Spine-tingling
thriller. ISBN 1-56280-120-1 10.95

NORTHERN BLUE by Tracey Richardson. 224 pp. Police recruits
Miki & Miranda — passion in the line of fire. ISBN 1-56280-118-X 10.95

LOVE'S HARVEST by Peggy J. Herring. 176 pp. by the author of
Once More With Feeling. ISBN 1-56280-117-1 10.95

THE COLOR OF WINTER by Lisa Shapiro. 208 pp. Romantic
love beyond your wildest dreams. ISBN 1-56280-116-3 10.95

FAMILY SECRETS by Laura DeHart Young. 208 pp. Enthralling
romance and suspense. ISBN 1-56280-119-8 10.95

INLAND PASSAGE by Jane Rule. 288 pp. Tales exploring conventional & unconventional relationships. ISBN 0-930044-56-8   10.95

DOUBLE BLUFF by Claire McNab. 208 pp. 7th Carol Ashton Mystery. ISBN 1-56280-096-5   10.95

BAR GIRLS by Lauran Hoffman. 176 pp. See the movie, read the book! ISBN 1-56280-115-5   10.95

THE FIRST TIME EVER edited by Barbara Grier & Christine Cassidy. 272 pp. Love stories by Naiad Press authors. ISBN 1-56280-086-8   14.95

MISS PETTIBONE AND MISS McGRAW by Brenda Weathers. 208 pp. A charming ghostly love story. ISBN 1-56280-151-1   10.95

CHANGES by Jackie Calhoun. 208 pp. Involved romance and relationships. ISBN 1-56280-083-3   10.95

FAIR PLAY by Rose Beecham. 256 pp. 3rd Amanda Valentine Mystery. ISBN 1-56280-081-7   10.95

PAYBACK by Celia Cohen. 176 pp. A gripping thriller of romance, revenge and betrayal. ISBN 1-56280-084-1   10.95

THE BEACH AFFAIR by Barbara Johnson. 224 pp. Sizzling summer romance/mystery/intrigue. ISBN 1-56280-090-6   10.95

GETTING THERE by Robbi Sommers. 192 pp. Nobody does it like Robbi! ISBN 1-56280-099-X   10.95

FINAL CUT by Lisa Haddock. 208 pp. 2nd Carmen Ramirez Mystery. ISBN 1-56280-088-4   10.95

FLASHPOINT by Katherine V. Forrest. 256 pp. A Lesbian blockbuster! ISBN 1-56280-079-5   11.95

CLAIRE OF THE MOON by Nicole Conn. Audio Book —Read by Marianne Hyatt. ISBN 1-56280-113-9   16.95

FOR LOVE AND FOR LIFE: INTIMATE PORTRAITS OF LESBIAN COUPLES by Susan Johnson. 224 pp. ISBN 1-56280-091-4   14.95

DEVOTION by Mindy Kaplan. 192 pp. See the movie — read the book! ISBN 1-56280-093-0   10.95

SOMEONE TO WATCH by Jaye Maiman. 272 pp. 4th Robin Miller Mystery. ISBN 1-56280-095-7   10.95

GREENER THAN GRASS by Jennifer Fulton. 208 pp. A young woman — a stranger in her bed. ISBN 1-56280-092-2   10.95

TRAVELS WITH DIANA HUNTER by Regine Sands. Erotic lesbian romp. Audio Book (2 cassettes) ISBN 1-56280-107-4   16.95

CABIN FEVER by Carol Schmidt. 256 pp. Sizzling suspense and passion. ISBN 1-56280-089-1   10.95

THERE WILL BE NO GOODBYES by Laura DeHart Young. 192 pp. Romantic love, strength, and friendship. ISBN 1-56280-103-1   10.95

FAULTLINE by Sheila Ortiz Taylor. 144 pp. Joyous comic
lesbian novel.   ISBN 1-56280-108-2   9.95

OPEN HOUSE by Pat Welch. 176 pp. 4th Helen Black Mystery.
         ISBN 1-56280-102-3   10.95

ONCE MORE WITH FEELING by Peggy J. Herring. 240 pp.
Lighthearted, loving romantic adventure.   ISBN 1-56280-089-2   11.95

FOREVER by Evelyn Kennedy. 224 pp. Passionate romance — love
overcoming all obstacles.   ISBN 1-56280-094-9   10.95

WHISPERS by Kris Bruyer. 176 pp. Romantic ghost story
         ISBN 1-56280-082-5   10.95

NIGHT SONGS by Penny Mickelbury. 224 pp. 2nd Gianna Maglione
Mystery.   ISBN 1-56280-097-3   10.95

GETTING TO THE POINT by Teresa Stores. 256 pp. Classic
southern Lesbian novel.   ISBN 1-56280-100-7   10.95

PAINTED MOON by Karin Kallmaker. 224 pp. Delicious
Kallmaker romance.   ISBN 1-56280-075-2   11.95

THE MYSTERIOUS NAIAD edited by Katherine V. Forrest &
Barbara Grier. 320 pp. Love stories by Naiad Press authors.
         ISBN 1-56280-074-4   14.95

DAUGHTERS OF A CORAL DAWN by Katherine V. Forrest.
240 pp. Tenth Anniversay Edition.   ISBN 1-56280-104-X   11.95

BODY GUARD by Claire McNab. 208 pp. 6th Carol Ashton
Mystery.   ISBN 1-56280-073-6   11.95

CACTUS LOVE by Lee Lynch. 192 pp. Stories by the beloved
storyteller.   ISBN 1-56280-071-X   9.95

SECOND GUESS by Rose Beecham. 216 pp. 2nd Amanda Valentine
Mystery.   ISBN 1-56280-069-8   9.95

A RAGE OF MAIDENS by Lauren Wright Douglas. 240 pp. 6th Caitlin
Reece Mystery.   ISBN 1-56280-068-X   10.95

TRIPLE EXPOSURE by Jackie Calhoun. 224 pp. Romantic drama
involving many characters.   ISBN 1-56280-067-1   10.95

UP, UP AND AWAY by Catherine Ennis. 192 pp. Delightful
romance.   ISBN 1-56280-065-5   11.95

PERSONAL ADS by Robbi Sommers. 176 pp. Sizzling short
stories.   ISBN 1-56280-059-0   11.95

CROSSWORDS by Penny Sumner. 256 pp. 2nd Victoria Cross
Mystery.   ISBN 1-56280-064-7   9.95

SWEET CHERRY WINE by Carol Schmidt. 224 pp. A novel of
suspense.   ISBN 1-56280-063-9   9.95

CERTAIN SMILES by Dorothy Tell. 160 pp. Erotic short stories.
         ISBN 1-56280-066-3   9.95

EDITED OUT by Lisa Haddock. 224 pp. 1st Carmen Ramirez
Mystery.   ISBN 1-56280-077-9   9.95

WEDNESDAY NIGHTS by Camarin Grae. 288 pp. Sexy
adventure.   ISBN 1-56280-060-4   10.95

SMOKEY O by Celia Cohen. 176 pp. Relationships on the
playing field.   ISBN 1-56280-057-4   9.95

KATHLEEN O'DONALD by Penny Hayes. 256 pp. Rose and
Kathleen find each other and employment in 1909 NYC.
                                             ISBN 1-56280-070-1   9.95

STAYING HOME by Elisabeth Nonas. 256 pp. Molly and Alix
want a baby . . . or do they?   ISBN 1-56280-076-0   10.95

TRUE LOVE by Jennifer Fulton. 240 pp. Six lesbians searching
for love in all the "right" places.   ISBN 1-56280-035-3   10.95

KEEPING SECRETS by Penny Mickelbury. 208 pp. 1st Gianna
Maglione Mystery.   ISBN 1-56280-052-3   9.95

THE ROMANTIC NAIAD edited by Katherine V. Forrest &
Barbara Grier. 336 pp. Love stories by Naiad Press authors.
                                             ISBN 1-56280-054-X   14.95

UNDER MY SKIN by Jaye Maiman. 336 pp. 3rd Robin Miller
Mystery.   ISBN 1-56280-049-3.   10.95

CAR POOL by Karin Kallmaker. 272pp. Lesbians on wheels
and then some!   ISBN 1-56280-048-5   10.95

NOT TELLING MOTHER: STORIES FROM A LIFE by Diane
Salvatore. 176 pp. Her 3rd novel.   ISBN 1-56280-044-2   9.95

GOBLIN MARKET by Lauren Wright Douglas. 240pp. 5th Caitlin
Reece Mystery.   ISBN 1-56280-047-7   10.95

LONG GOODBYES by Nikki Baker. 256 pp. 3rd Virginia Kelly
Mystery.   ISBN 1-56280-042-6   9.95

FRIENDS AND LOVERS by Jackie Calhoun. 224 pp. Mid-
western Lesbian lives and loves.   ISBN 1-56280-041-8   11.95

THE CAT CAME BACK by Hilary Mullins. 208 pp. Highly
praised Lesbian novel.   ISBN 1-56280-040-X   9.95

BEHIND CLOSED DOORS by Robbi Sommers. 192 pp. Hot,
erotic short stories.   ISBN 1-56280-039-6   11.95

CLAIRE OF THE MOON by Nicole Conn. 192 pp. See the
movie — read the book!   ISBN 1-56280-038-8   10.95

SILENT HEART by Claire McNab. 192 pp. Exotic Lesbian
romance.   ISBN 1-56280-036-1   11.95

THE SPY IN QUESTION by Amanda Kyle Williams. 256 pp.
4th Madison McGuire Mystery.   ISBN 1-56280-037-X   9.95

SAVING GRACE by Jennifer Fulton. 240 pp. Adventure and
romantic entanglement.   ISBN 1-56280-051-5   10.95

CURIOUS WINE by Katherine V. Forrest. 176 pp. Tenth Anniversary Edition. The most popular contemporary Lesbian love story.
ISBN 1-56280-053-1 11.95
Audio Book (2 cassettes) ISBN 1-56280-105-8 16.95

CHAUTAUQUA by Catherine Ennis. 192 pp. Exciting, romantic adventure. ISBN 1-56280-032-9 9.95

A PROPER BURIAL by Pat Welch. 192 pp. 3rd Helen Black Mystery. ISBN 1-56280-033-7 9.95

SILVERLAKE HEAT: A Novel of Suspense by Carol Schmidt. 240 pp. Rhonda is as hot as Laney's dreams. ISBN 1-56280-031-0 9.95

LOVE, ZENA BETH by Diane Salvatore. 224 pp. The most talked about lesbian novel of the nineties! ISBN 1-56280-030-2 10.95

A DOORYARD FULL OF FLOWERS by Isabel Miller. 160 pp. Stories incl. 2 sequels to Patience and Sarah. ISBN 1-56280-029-9 9.95

MURDER BY TRADITION by Katherine V. Forrest. 288 pp. 4th Kate Delafield Mystery. ISBN 1-56280-002-7 11.95

THE EROTIC NAIAD edited by Katherine V. Forrest & Barbara Grier. 224 pp. Love stories by Naiad Press authors.
ISBN 1-56280-026-4 14.95

DEAD CERTAIN by Claire McNab. 224 pp. 5th Carol Ashton Mystery. ISBN 1-56280-027-2 10.95

CRAZY FOR LOVING by Jaye Maiman. 320 pp. 2nd Robin Miller Mystery. ISBN 1-56280-025-6 10.95

STONEHURST by Barbara Johnson. 176 pp. Passionate regency romance. ISBN 1-56280-024-8 9.95

INTRODUCING AMANDA VALENTINE by Rose Beecham. 256 pp. 1st Amanda Valentine Mystery. ISBN 1-56280-021-3 10.95

UNCERTAIN COMPANIONS by Robbi Sommers. 204 pp. Steamy, erotic novel. ISBN 1-56280-017-5 11.95

A TIGER'S HEART by Lauren W. Douglas. 240 pp. 4th Caitlin Reece Mystery. ISBN 1-56280-018-3 9.95

PAPERBACK ROMANCE by Karin Kallmaker. 256 pp. A delicious romance. ISBN 1-56280-019-1 10.95

THE LAVENDER HOUSE MURDER by Nikki Baker. 224 pp. 2nd Virginia Kelly Mystery. ISBN 1-56280-012-4 9.95

PASSION BAY by Jennifer Fulton. 224 pp. Passionate romance, virgin beaches, tropical skies. ISBN 1-56280-028-0 10.95

STICKS AND STONES by Jackie Calhoun. 208 pp. Contemporary lesbian lives and loves. ISBN 1-56280-020-5 9.95
Audio Book (2 cassettes) ISBN 1-56280-106-6 16.95

UNDER THE SOUTHERN CROSS by Claire McNab. 192 pp. Romantic nights Down Under. ISBN 1-56280-011-6 11.95

GRASSY FLATS by Penny Hayes. 256 pp. Lesbian romance in
the '30s.   ISBN 1-56280-010-8   9.95

A SINGULAR SPY by Amanda K. Williams. 192 pp. 3rd
Madison McGuire Mystery.   ISBN 1-56280-008-6   8.95

THE END OF APRIL by Penny Sumner. 240 pp. 1st Victoria
Cross Mystery.   ISBN 1-56280-007-8   8.95

KISS AND TELL by Robbi Sommers. 192 pp. Scorching stories
by the author of *Pleasures.*   ISBN 1-56280-005-1   11.95

STILL WATERS by Pat Welch. 208 pp. 2nd Helen Black Mystery.
                                               ISBN 0-941483-97-5   9.95

TO LOVE AGAIN by Evelyn Kennedy. 208 pp. Wildly romantic
love story.   ISBN 0-941483-85-1   11.95

IN THE GAME by Nikki Baker. 192 pp. 1st Virginia Kelly
Mystery.   ISBN 1-56280-004-3   9.95

STRANDED by Camarin Grae. 320 pp. Entertaining, riveting
adventure.   ISBN 0-941483-99-1   9.95

THE DAUGHTERS OF ARTEMIS by Lauren Wright Douglas.
240 pp. 3rd Caitlin Reece Mystery.   ISBN 0-941483-95-9   9.95

CLEARWATER by Catherine Ennis. 176 pp. Romantic secrets
of a small Louisiana town.   ISBN 0-941483-65-7   8.95

THE HALLELUJAH MURDERS by Dorothy Tell. 176 pp. 2nd
Poppy Dillworth Mystery.   ISBN 0-941483-88-6   8.95

SECOND CHANCE by Jackie Calhoun. 256 pp. Contemporary
Lesbian lives and loves.   ISBN 0-941483-93-2   9.95

BENEDICTION by Diane Salvatore. 272 pp. Striking, contemporary romantic novel.   ISBN 0-941483-90-8   11.95

TOUCHWOOD by Karin Kallmaker. 240 pp. Loving, May/
December romance.   ISBN 0-941483-76-2   11.95

COP OUT by Claire McNab. 208 pp. 4th Carol Ashton Mystery.
                                               ISBN 0-941483-84-3   10.95

THE BEVERLY MALIBU by Katherine V. Forrest. 288 pp. 3rd
Kate Delafield Mystery.   ISBN 0-941483-48-7   11.95

THE PROVIDENCE FILE by Amanda Kyle Williams. 256 pp.
2nd Madison McGuire Mystery.   ISBN 0-941483-92-4   8.95

I LEFT MY HEART by Jaye Maiman. 320 pp. 1st Robin Miller
Mystery.   ISBN 0-941483-72-X   10.95

THE PRICE OF SALT by Patricia Highsmith (writing as Claire
Morgan). 288 pp. Classic lesbian novel, first issued in 1952 . . .
acknowledged by its author under her own, very famous, name.
                                               ISBN 1-56280-003-5   10.95

SIDE BY SIDE by Isabel Miller. 256 pp. From beloved author of
Patience and Sarah.   ISBN 0-941483-77-0   10.95